The Fly Who
Knew Too Much

a comic novel

To Bryce and Jack (e; good clients and even better friends

[signature]

By
M. Taylor

CONTENTS

CONTENTS

Chapter 1
A Fly is Born

I am the fly on the wall, the lowly insect nobody notices when a person vents their anger, slanders the boss, cheats on the spouse, or lies to friends. If I could speak, I could tell you things you never imagined, straight from the lips and loins of the famous, the infamous, the revered, and the reviled. I am no ordinary fruit fly, drosophila melanogaster, the most studied of all the insects - but a mutant.

Mutants among flies are not uncommon. Some have more feet, some have more wings, some have different colored eyes and others have different body formations. The list is endless. While I can't totally explain my oddness, I have been a witness to people's behavior that is every bit as unusual as my own condition.

Experience tells me that those who report and reflect on the human condition cannot be trusted to tell it like it is. Historians, journalists, novelists, bloggers, academics, memoirists, and biographers; all are suspect. Unless they were on that wall, or in the room, guesswork and speculation rule the day, and flights of fantasy rule the night. The truth is bent to serve the author's needs. Accuracy is a casualty of attitude. These chroniclers are human, and all have a motive, a point to make, an ax to grind, or a dollar to earn. Not so with me or any other fly.

My diet, birth, and all other circumstances were very different from the norm. I was born in a dumpster behind Gelson's market in Calabasas, California, one of roughly 600 eggs fertilized and hatched there at the same time. Imagine 600 siblings for starters. Think of that crowd right out of the gate. Good luck remembering their nameless faces.

The fruit fly is fertile within about twelve hours after hatching. It's like being born a teenager with all the hormones raging, no life experience to fall back on, total freedom to fly anywhere then skid-land on some other creature's turf, and no one to guide or caution you. Think of a mindless teenager attempting to copulate, uninvited, with a mature member of the opposite sex while she's foraging for food. Welcome to the world of the fly - my world.

Our life cycle is often shorter because of two forces that collide like speeding trains: careless flies vs. dangerous, irritable humans. It takes luck to cope with this lethal combination. We just want sex and food, not unlike the teenagers we resemble hormonally. We don't care where or when we get it. At least humans are a trifle more disciplined, if not discerning. The number of flies killed every day borders on genocide. But if you only have thirty days to live you too would be jittery and frantic to get on with it, eager to stuff yourself whenever a meal came along, then strut your stuff like a horny teen on steroids.

I was lucky right from the start. On my first day out of the dumpster, I looked around at my new world, starting with the Gelson's parking lot. The first object I approached was a machine on four wheels the color of a banana. I learned soon that it was an automobile called a Mercedes-Benz convertible. Its mistress, who sat behind the wheel, was a beautiful, young blonde woman. She started the machine with a ferocious roar that nearly blew out my hearing. I flew into the car through a partly opened window without the woman noticing me, drawn by the scent of a bag of fruit.

She pulled out of the parking lot, an open bag of groceries on the rear seat of the car containing a half-eaten apple in the bag with me all over it. I hugged the floor mat while she drove across the steep hills to her home.

I kept silent, working on the apple, which was nothing short of miraculous.

Blonde woman: "Malibu, at last." She looked out over the water and brought the machine to a stop.

I hid in the grocery bag and she carried me into her house. She unloaded the bag onto a kitchen counter but was interrupted by a phone call. I slipped out of the bag and was free to observe her clean and colorful house with windows looking out to the ocean, the rooms bathed in the light of day. I knew instantly that I had landed in a stunning location.

I would do anything to remain here no matter what the risk. I would make this my home.

Chapter 2
Early Education

When my girl returned to the kitchen, she unloaded the bag of fruit into a large boxy structure. The open door emitted a rush of cold air. If I had stayed with the fruit, I would have been instantly frozen to death. More good fortune followed as I noticed a small open door to a pantry containing harmless-looking items, like brooms and mops. I slipped into the space where I could hide when necessary and even sleep.

I shouldn't get too carried away, but this girl was as beautiful and juicy as the first apple I landed on. Leaving was not an option after I had tasted that lovely Gelson's fruit which she brought home by the bucket load. I settled into this magical environment, coming out of the closet, as I called it, to explore carefully the lifestyle of my host without making a nuisance of myself. After a short time, I could not picture myself dumpster diving for food, surrounded by hordes of flies that I was expected to service or befriend. There was no choice, I would have to cast my fate with humanity.

But even a fly gets enough food sometimes, and needs to do more than eat to fill up the time. I learned how to use this strange thing that happened to my brain that allowed me to understand the language of the humans I was exposed to. I eavesdropped on phone and personal conversations, watched television, looked at magazines, listened to the radio, and visitors in my host's house. My education began early as I learned the habits and interests of the humans who surrounded me, thereby cheating the odds that I would be discovered and dispatched without my consent.

My host - at first, I merely called her my girl. I learned from eavesdropping on her telephone conversations that her name was Barbara.

She lived by herself and spent a lot of time at home. Often, she had her clothes off or wore very few pieces of fabric. I gained an appreciation for the human anatomy, but I also saw how people behaved differently with their clothing on. When Barbara went without clothes, she looked as open, free, and playful as the wind, or the water. When she wore clothes, not so free.

The choice, to say nothing of the accompanying rituals, of what to wear for each occasion, seemed to alter her human personality. Not a problem we flies have to contend with. Insects are stuck with what they have, naked to the world. The luxury of disguise, as I learned, is a purely human trait. It makes life very confusing, as people are not always what they appear to be, and they like it that way.

As time passed, Barbara seemed to tolerate me as an insignificant part of her universe. At times, I would approach her quietly, drawn by the sweet odor she threw off, like the fruit we both ate so much of. When she was distracted by a book, a magazine, or the flat-screen television, I would quietly settle as close to her as possible, but looking for the opportunity to land near one of her breasts. They were so soft and lovely that I would forget about food, the company of other flies, and even the danger that she might swat and kill me instantly if I lingered too long in the sweet fog of her scent.

A frequent guest in the house was a male human named Adam. He had much shorter hair and was taller and more muscular than Barbara. She sometimes called him her boyfriend. I could not understand her fascination with this person, who often appeared in shabby clothes, drank tons of beer, and watched meaningless television shows of men and women who fought one another in roped-off rings, steel cages, or parking lots.

I gathered from their conversations that she and Adam belonged to an acting class (whatever that is) in which Barbara was the acknowledged star and Adam was the handsome dunce.

He was punished by the other class members and the teacher, all of whom criticized him and teased him mercilessly. Softhearted Barbara comforted him and even invited him to study with her outside the class at her home. Once there he and Barbara did what all young and beautiful people apparently do with one another. Engage in sex.

Adam came to the house mostly in the evening, on a large two-wheeled apparatus called a Harley-Davidson motorcycle. He revered the machine and pestered Barbara to ride with him on the back of the single-seat, her arms wrapped around him. She begged off more than she rode because he was drinking and she feared for her safety. Whatever money Adam had from odd jobs he spent on buying the bike and maintaining it. He never had money to buy food, beer, or decent clothes, relying on Barbara to provide for him. I saw him as a leech, a blood-sucking parasite.

From time to time the two of them would argue about minor issues and then make up. Making up usually meant sex. At first, I thought they were in a physical fight, and I feared for Barbara's safety, yet she was never injured. She seemed to enjoy some of the flailing and commotion as they shed clothing and inhibitions, even when they locked together like some dogs on the beach I had witnessed.

I was excluded from much of the sex because it took place in the bedroom behind a closed door. Often when they came out of the bedroom Barbara would bring out a script and coax Adam into preparing for a scene they were to perform in class. She had to explain the motivation of the characters to Adam, the meaning of the dialogue, the movements, and the gestures of the actors as they spoke.

He rarely grasped her instructions, standing immobile and slurring the words he read. When he did move, he was stiff, like a statue on wheels, with no facial expressions or body language to give life to the written words. It was obvious that Adam, handsome as he was, had no future as an actor.

The rehearsal would be interrupted by Adam's effort to move Barbara back to the bedroom for more sex. If she resisted, he headed to the refrigerator for a beer or two, often a snack left over from dinner. She didn't always refuse; she liked the sex until it felt like she was a captive to Adam's obsession with sex above all.

If I had a voice, I could have told Barbara that she was wasting her time with Adam. He had no thoughts or ideas of his own, just those that Barbara tried, mostly unsuccessful, to plant in him. He lacked education, charm, taste, money, awareness, and ambition, all characteristics that Barbara considered important. I wished fervently that I could morph into a prince, or just a guy in his twenties with a job, exactly like one of those fairy tales, or movies where the underling emerges from his temporary condition to pursue the fair maiden of his dreams.

The only thing I could admire about Adam was his lack of curiosity and his minimal awareness of my presence in the house. I would have to wait until Barbara was tired of his antics and saw him for the disaster that he was, despite his well-formed face, his outstanding abs, and his thick head of fair hair. There was nothing I could do about Adam and his relationship with Barbara, which I saw as tenuous at best. I would have to learn patience, a nearly impossible task for a common fruit fly, and as I learned, most humans.

Barbara was far too much for Adam to comprehend and she would never settle for him. Of that, I was certain.

Chapter 3
Exit Adam

My attitude toward Adam didn't count for much as the silent, hidden partner in the triangular set-up of Barbara's house. She continued to tolerate his obvious faults and defects. Their active sex life kept the relationship alive, at least for a time, as did his dependence on Barbara, and his worship of her body. He could not keep his hands off her, in particular her creamy breasts. Nor could he stop talking about them, as though they were separate beings from the rest of her. "Golden apples" he called them, nuzzling her breasts whether they were exposed or clothed. Barbara was amused by his clumsy attention, except when he had too many beers and exhibited the classic signs of a hopeless drunk.

One evening, after they emerged from the closed-door bedroom, they sat facing one another at the kitchen table. Barbara was nursing her first beer of the night and Adam was on his fourth. I observed his passage from the bedroom, doing the drunkard's heavy-footed dance, lurching down the hallway as if it were a moving footbridge.

I guessed that things in the bedroom had not gone well. Normally, they came out smiling and teasing one another. The mood this night was different.

Barbara: "You need to lighten up on the drinking Adam. You know why."

Adam: "Okay, I didn't do so good tonight. It never happened before."

Barbara: "It isn't just tonight, and it has happened before. You've been showing up drunk at our acting class. You haven't memorized your lines; you don't follow directions. You'll never learn to be an actor if you keep it up."

Adam: "So what? There are a million other things I can do. I don't have to be an actor."

Barbara: "What is it you really want to do?"

Adam: "I want to race motorcycles, race stock cars, and fly planes. Lots of things."

Barbara: "You can't drink and do races or fly airplanes. You'll kill someone, maybe yourself if you're drunk. You will never be hired or paid by anyone if you drink too much."

Adam: "You're always telling me what to do. You don't know everything. You're not perfect, nobody's perfect."

Barbara: (irritated) "Go ahead, tell me what I'm doing wrong."

Adam stared into his beer, looking for an answer that wasn't there, and would never be. "I'm sorry, I shouldn't have said that. I'm kind of stressed right now because I don't like the acting class. I'm no good at it, and I'm quitting.

Barbara: "It takes time and practice to get it right. You have to give it more time."

Adam: "It costs too much and I'm broke. I need to make some money, and I have some offers. Do you remember Dan, the guy who dropped out of the class a couple of months ago?"

Barbara: "I do. He kept asking me to go with him to Palm Springs, or Las Vegas for a weekend. I had no interest in Dan. I found him to be sleazy and boring."

Adam: "He was about my only friend in the class. He called me about some deals and some work for me to earn some easy money.

Barbara: "What kind of deals and what kind of work?"

Adam: "I don't want to tell you. You won't like it."

Barbara: "Is it something illegal?"

Adam: "Not exactly."

Barbara: "Is Dan doing the kind of work you're thinking about?"

Adam: "Kind of. I'm not sure. He doesn't say too much, just that the money's good and the work is easy. He auditions for parts in adult films and gets a role that pays him in cash, and there's no waiting around. It's done fast and he's done.

He says they like him, and he's getting roles where he doesn't have to audition so much. He has to look good, so he works out when he isn't filming. He says the industry is cranking out money for everyone, and that it's far bigger and better than the regular film industry. He didn't need any acting class, just his good looks and ability to have sex on camera with pretty girls. He told me most of his friends were jealous and would trade places with him in a New York minute.

Barbara: "Did you really consider doing this sex work, and still maintain a relationship with me? How do you think I would feel about having sex with you after you had been with different women all day long?"

Adam: "Dan tells me that most of the women performers are married and the husbands help with their careers. They do photography, check all the medications and doctor appointments to make sure they don't have any disease, and work out with them to make sure they look good. They say it's just a job, doing what they would do at home, and it's nothing to be ashamed of."

Barbara: "Adam, your idea is a non-starter for me. What kind of other deals does Dan have you interested in?"

Adam: "Two things. One is being an escort, taking older women to parties, charity events, and things. I don't have to have sex with them, just look good and be polite."

Barbara: "We're already in the basement of life with these plans. Is there anything else? What's the last proposal?"

Adam: "Dan says he needs another five thousand to swing a purchase of some really first-rate cocaine which he can sell overnight without any risk to himself. If I had the money, I could double it in a week."

Barbara: "Has Dan told you what the penalties are if you're caught selling cocaine?"

Adam: "No."

Barbara: "When you go home tonight, google penalties in California for the sale of cocaine."

Adam: "I thought I would stay here tonight. We could look it up on your computer. Mine crashed on me weeks ago."

Barbara: "Adam, you should go home now. I feel dirty just talking about this stuff, and if you are serious about any one of these plans then we can't be together. It's that simple."

Adam looked like he wanted to cry.

Barbara: "You need to sober up before you go. I won't push you out until I'm satisfied that you won't get in an accident on your motorcycle. You need to get a handle on your drinking, which has reached the point of no return. AA would be a place to get you straightened out before you go any further down the road you just told me about.

It doesn't cost anything at AA. You can't use money as an excuse not to do it."

Barbara made some strong coffee and sat with him while he drank two large cups. There wasn't much left to say, except for Barbara to emphasize that Adam should not be climbing onto his Harley before he was sobered up.

Adam:(trying to rally) "Got any other advice for me since you know me so well?"

Barbara: "Stay away from Dan."

I was pinned to the kitchen wall listening to this conversation. I knew that Adam's half-baked, ill-considered schemes were fatal to any further relationship with Barbara. I would not miss him and ultimately Barbara would be better off without him. However, I did feel sorry for him. It was brutal the way he was self-destructing.

I had heard Barbara's girlfriends talking with her on the phone, saying that beautiful women were often crazy about bad boys - the unconventional ones who lived by their own rules. Human relationships have unwritten rules, but Adam shouldn't need written rules to realize that he had gone too far.

He already allowed Barbara to buy him clothes, supply food and beer, and give him cash when he asked for it. Now he proposed to break the unwritten rules of a relationship for nothing more than the right to self-destruct in the slippery worlds of pornography and drugs.

If the television therapists were right, bad boys were just a phase. It was puzzling to me that Barbara, who seemed so mature, would want to be stuck with such a juvenile, even dangerous character.

She barely had time to miss him, once he was gone. Her career was ramping up with constant appearances on television shows, interviews, auditions, reading scripts for movie parts, and meeting with producers and directors.

Adam was not immediately replaced by other men. On some evenings, Barbara would take a velvet-lined box from her bedroom night table, remove a shiny cylindrical object that made a buzzing sound (like a frightened fly), and insert it between her legs. She whipped her blonde hair back and forth, moaning softly, while I lingered on the lace curtain that covered her bedroom window.

After she convulsed, she settled back and slept. She must have forgotten that I was lurking about, or she would have closed the bedroom door. I felt like a voyeur at first, but I got over it, because it helped me to learn that men like Adam were not the only source of pleasure for women.

Chapter 4
Discovery

One day when Barbara and I were alone in the house, she seemed to be watching me carefully. She looked directly at me and spoke to me for the first time.

Barbara: "We need to talk."

She reached into the pantry closet and withdrew a cylindrical object with a picture of a housefly, two black bands crossed over the image of a fly.

Barbara: "This is a poison spray, and it could kill you instantly if I chose to use it on you. I won't use it on you, but only if you answer my questions and tell the truth. If you lie to me, I won't hesitate. Do you understand me?"

I said nothing, of course, because I could not.

Barbara: "I know this is crazy but I think you are watching me, living with me. I can't believe I am talking to a fly. I must be crazy."

She shook her beautiful head and stamped her feet, seemingly at a loss for words.

Barbara: "You can't possibly understand, that's just too much. I must be having a Zoloft withdrawal."

I had no idea what that meant. I held my ground, waiting to see what she would do next. She went for a glass of wine in her refrigerator. When the phone rang, she answered it. Actors reflexively answer the phone because it might be an agent calling with news for or from an audition or a role becoming available. Too late, she recognized Adam on her caller ID.

She punched the button on her smartphone to end the call. She reached for another glass of wine, finished it off, and filled up a third glass. She waved the spray can at me to make sure it had not been forgotten. I was frightened beyond words. There was no way I could lie to her, even if I wanted to do so. I might have considered making a run for my life had I not been so frightened by the outside world. I was now facing the most awful fate. Murdered by the one I loved.

I elected to stay put. If the end was near, so be it. Maybe I aspired to heights that could never be reached. I should have been satisfied to be a harmless scavenger, or at most an inglorious pest.

Barbara: "If you understand me, fly over to the pastel green suede sofa and land on the middle cushion. Stay there until I tell you where to go next."

I wasn't sure whether I should expose myself so I did nothing. She hesitated for a moment, then turned and sprayed a shot of poison away toward the kitchen. It caused her to sneeze.

When her reaction stopped, she started in on me again.

Barbara: "Goddamn you, you must be a male fly. Men just clam up when you want to talk to them. They turn into statues or they get so angry they can't talk at all so they leave or get drunk. Too drunk to face the emotional music. They're relationship cowards, and so are you. That's what you are. You chicken shit fly, damn you. You've been watching me, eating my food, even landing on me because you want to feel me up. You like it, don't you? You filthy insect, do something or get out. Get out, you miserable, stinking voyeur. You're so much like the other men I've known; it makes me sick."

She threw open the door and tried to chase me out, but I wouldn't go, which infuriated her further. Now she was screaming at me, loud enough so that her next-door neighbor came out of her place and asked if everything was all right.

Barbara: (to neighbor) "It's all right, it's okay. I just fly off the handle sometimes."

She closed the door and addressed me again.

Barbara: "Do you see what you made me do? This is all your fault. What if she called the cops? What do I say to them? I'm pissed off at my pet fly? He won't do what I tell him to do. I'll be locked up. My career goes up in smoke. It's not like I'm Kim Kardashian or Pamela Anderson. They do sex films, have tons of boyfriends, get in accidents, and nobody cares. Other women are alcoholics or drug users. It's no big deal. They go to rehab, and everybody understands.

But me, if I get busted for talking to flies; nobody understands that. Hell, I wouldn't understand."

I couldn't stand it, so I flew over to the pastel green suede sofa and landed on the middle cushion. She stopped and waited.

Barbara: "Okay, fly over to the window and wait on the window sill."

I flew over to the window sill and waited. She looked really confused.

Barbara: (muttering) "This can't be happening. Maybe I should go on SNL with my trained fly. I can hear the bad jokes already about me and flies. 'She can train my fly anytime.' 'This woman really knows her way around a fly.' 'She can make your fly do tricks you never dreamed of'."

I waited because I couldn't think of anything else to do. She seemed to calm down some, but I wasn't sure. I had very little experience with women, and it was not as though I could talk to her and tell her what I was thinking. I didn't know how I could be useful to her, or how to be a valued asset of some kind. Beyond that, I was no more than a curiosity, a freak, a mutant insect, a misfit with no purpose in life, a stranger in her world who could never be explained.

Barbara: (conversationally) "What are you doing over there? Probably feeling sorry for yourself, like most men I know. I can see the way you hang your head and fold your wings. Well, at least I don't have to stroke you or kiss you to make you feel better. You just have to get it together on your own, live with your male pride the best you can."

She was right. I was feeling sorry for myself. I needed to prove to her that I could do something useful, only she was the one who needed to find a means to that end. I could not plant that thought in her head. She had to figure it out for herself. We needed to communicate with one another. While I could not talk, I could buzz for starters, so I flew onto a piece of fruit, a banana to be exact.

Barbara: "Are you hungry?"

I buzzed as loud as I could. I nodded my head, but I don't believe she got that. Without a neck, my head doesn't move much.

Barbara: "If you are hungry buzz twice, as loud as you can."

I gave off two very loud buzzes. She peeled the banana, and I got down to the business of eating. She waited, thinking up another test for me. We went on like this for some time, her asking questions for me to answer with one, two buzzes, or three buzzes. She would direct me to fly somewhere, land on something; little intelligence tests. She was at least satisfied enough to put the poison spray back in the pantry where I had made a shelter for myself.

She calmed down, sat in her favorite chair, and opened a glossy magazine to which she subscribed. She flipped the pages, looking for different sections to give her ideas. In the lifestyle section, she saw a photograph of an older man standing next to a magnificent reddish-brown horse ridden by a smaller man, seated on a saddle wearing a bright silk shirt and high leather boots.

Barbara: "That's it!"

She did not explain what she meant, although she was pleased with herself. She continued to read the magazine and glanced at me occasionally. I flew to a place where I could see what she was reading from the magazine. She nodded and smiled.

Barbara: "Fly, how would you like to come to work with me tomorrow? I will be making a guest appearance on a nationally televised show. Buzz twice if you want to go."

I buzzed excitedly at the chance to emerge into the outside world and see Barbara perform in a real show.

Barbara: "You will have to be inconspicuous and not give away our secret that you understand me, or anyone else. You will have to be careful at all times and hide from people and remain at a distance from me. I will be busy getting made up, then costumed, maybe a bite to eat before I enter the show, and then lunch with my agent before we return home.

If you run into trouble I can't help you, I can only do so much before our secret is blown. You won't be able to go with me and my agent for lunch, so you will have to find food for yourself if you need it. I'll have food in the car when we head back to Malibu, probably some leftovers from lunch.

She didn't say much more. She was in a good mood all night long, offering me food, putting out candy, watching television, and talking to me like I was a long-lost friend. I had far too much to eat and drink.

Perhaps to improve my mood, she surfed around the television channels until she found a sappy movie about a boy and his dog. She didn't know how I felt about dogs. I fell asleep in the middle of the movie on the green suede couch that was my first testing ground.

Chapter 5
Survival

Barbara rose early the next day. She didn't put on any makeup and was dressed in yoga pants and a matching cotton top, and rushed out, leaving me to follow her into the car.

I entered the car and rode with her, eager to experience her world. She drove over the hills, stopped at my birthplace for something she called a latte, and then emerged onto a large ribbon of concrete filled with other cars that drove headlong toward the rising sun at a blazing rate of speed.

She turned on the car radio and sang with the radio, then called some girlfriends on her cell phone. Men in other cars, also driving at high speeds, tried to make eye contact with her as they passed her or she passed them. They whistled, waved, nodded, or just stared; she seemed to like it, although there were some near collisions.

We arrived at a large, blocky building with the letters CBS on the front. A uniformed guard waved us in, and she parked her yellow car in a small space next to a separate building. I left the car with her, careful to follow at a distance. We slipped into the building where she then went directly to a room and was seated in an oversized chair facing a bank of mirrors.

Other women immediately began to apply creams and solutions to her face, fuss with her hair, paint above her eyes, and paste on her eyelashes all the while talking and gossiping with her, mostly about their boyfriends, in whining, snarling tones. I was surprised that she allowed these people to swarm all over her, changing her appearance, her hair and face with pots full of jelly-like goo.

She seemed untroubled and submitted to their ministrations. What possible reason was there to change this supremely beautiful face? When they finished with her, she peered carefully at the effect of all the changes, nodded her approval, and thanked the women warmly for their services. They had managed to make her even more beautiful; perfection, I would say, if I could speak.

There were men too, doing the same process with other women, but they managed to sound like the women; they too were fixated on their boyfriends. Were they faithful? Were they fat? Were they boring, broke, or obsessed with sports, gambling, booze, drugs, parties, clothes, and girls with big tits? Either their boyfriends worked all the time or they didn't work at all. They were high as kites or depressed beyond description. Barbara ignored these conversations boiling around her.

After what seemed like hours, Barbara rose and I flew behind her into another room where another group of women gave her clothing to try on. This process went on even longer than the first one, and I grew slightly bored. I must have given myself away. One of the younger women who had been searching through racks of clothing near the wall suddenly turned toward me, straightened up with a magazine in her hand, and slammed it against the wall. It clipped the edge of my wing. I was momentarily stunned, but reacted quickly to zoom away while she let loose a string of words and feelings that I had never heard before. I would hear them again.

Girl: "Goddamn fucking flies. I hate them. They're everywhere in the summer. This whole place is full of flies and bugs. They should spray this place every goddamn day. They've taken over everything here, we need to get rid of every last one."

I raced for the door, survival instincts kicking in, frightened that I would lose contact with Barbara and be lost in the maze of this huge building. I knew I could not go back to the costume room. Barbara left the room, telling the girl she needed a short break, and followed me out of the room. She pointed down the hallway and checked the corridor to make sure nobody was watching us.

Barbara: (whispering) "Cafeteria. Food that way."

She retreated to the costume room, and I flew as directed.

I entered a large room, at the base of a stairway down the hall far from the clothing room, where food was being served buffet-style at one end of the room.

The big room was crowded with men and women, some in costume, some all made up, talking and gesturing, often repeating the same sentences. They called this "rehearsing." They spoke in many different tones at different volumes. They were not whiny like the face painters and hair arrangers. Some of the speakers were forceful and convincing. Non-speakers buried their faces in loosely bound papers with large lettering, which they muttered over between bites of food. These were scripts, exactly like the ones Barbara read at home.

There was an abundance of uneaten food, and I helped myself at an abandoned table. I could have gorged myself all day long if I chose to, since most of the women paid no attention to their food and left far more on their plates than they ate. These women seemed abnormally thin, the skin of their necks, shoulder blades, collarbones, and arms stretched to the breaking point. I felt as though I did them a favor by eating their food.

There was one table, off by itself, composed of two youthful-looking men wearing tight clothing in abnormally bright colors and women in dark suits. Each person seemed bent on examining his or her food, but failed to eat most of it. There was much talk about food and things they called diets. I concluded diets must be the enemies of food, like magazines and newspapers are mine.

They bantered over what pills and supplements should be taken with the uneaten food. Nobody approached this table, which told me that they were a different caste within this larger group. One of the men wore shoulder-length blond hair, had delicate features, a sculpted jawline, and blue eyes, nearly as clear and piercing as Barbara's. He was almost as pretty. The others, even when talking to one another, glanced at him constantly, although they didn't want to be seen doing it. He was aware of the attention but seemed removed, even remote, while much of the conversation was directed at him.

Woman one: "Michael, are you playing golf with Tom today?" Michael nodded, his long blonde mane answering the question for him.

Woman two: "Are you playing at Lakeside?"

Michael: "No, we like the Trump course in Palos Verdes. When we finish, I can go down to my place in Laguna Beach."

Woman three: "I just love Laguna, it's so pretty. Are you in town or on the beach?"

Michael gave a half-smile and poked at his food without responding.

Woman one: "Golf takes so long to play, and you don't get any cardio benefit from it."

Woman two: "It's great for business, though. Where else can you get an A-list movie star or director all to yourself for three hours without his agent or lawyer horning in?"

Man two: "Michael told me his best trick. He has the caddy assigned to his guest to go through his golf bag and clean his clubs before they play. He finds and turns the power off on the cell phone. Otherwise, it rings non-stop."

Woman one: "Is that true Michael?"

Michael's hair answered for him again.

Woman two: "Brilliant. The next time I take a guest to my place in Aspen, I'll do the same thing."

Woman three: "Are you in town or on the hill? I just love it there."

I scratched the side of my eye with my back leg and thought, "Didn't she just say that?"

Woman one: "I won't be skiing this year. I'm shopping for a condo in St. Martin."

Michael's cell phone rang. He listened, hung up, and said, "No golf today. Tom has to meet with Steven. I think I'll go down to Laguna and work out at my club instead."

Woman two: "I'm up to an hour on the stair-master with hand weights and I lost three pounds this week alone."

Everyone at the table nodded and in unison, they all pushed their food away.

Later, I learned that these people were called executives. I gathered from their conversation that executives were expected to play golf at least once a week at their private golf clubs, ski in distant locations in the winter, drive only foreign cars, shop for designer clothes in exclusive boutiques, acquire excessive amounts of jewelry, own second homes in exotic tropical locations, and workout religiously in private clubs.

Maybe, if I were living with flies, I could be like this guy called Michael. How would I feel if my fellow flies saw me as some kind of deity? I'd be pumped up, self-infatuated, and the center of attention at all times. I'd have to think about this kind of goal; there had to be some negatives.

The conversation all but came to a halt when Barbara entered the room in full makeup and costume. She drew the attention of everyone in the room and seemed to bathe in it. I wanted to beat my wings together by way of applause. Even the executives interrupted their conversation for a moment to stare at her. She strolled past the executive table, slowing down to give them just a glimpse of her creamy breasts, pushed up by her low-cut dress. Then she turned away to exhibit her tight backside encased in a clinging material that melted onto her skin like it was laminated to her body.

She never made eye contact with them or acknowledged them as anything more than an audience. Everyone at the table nodded appreciatively as she took her seat at a table with two other young women in costumes. She winked at me as she sat down.

Man two: "That girl is hot. Hotter than a stolen boyfriend."

Woman one: "If I worked out every day for the next decade I could still not get into that dress."

Woman two: "What show is she on this morning?"

Woman three: "She's doing a guest turn on Y and R. I hear New York wants her to be a regular. She could be a star in the making."

Woman one: "What do you think Michael?"

Michael: "Who does her hair?"

When Barbara left the room, I followed at a comfortable distance as she walked down another hallway, this time to a far larger room filled with equipment, wires, lights, and more people. I heard one of them call this the sound stage.

There was a room within a room, filled with men and women who were made up and dressed in dark suits, black dresses, and glittering jewelry on their hands and about their necks. They were chattering away with one another and lifting bell-shaped glasses filled with a pale amber liquid that seemed to bubble.

A small, balding man, dressed in a faded T-shirt and jeans, gave orders and motioned people to either cluster or separate. Barbara plunged into this scene. From time to time she turned her head and faced one of the several cameras, speaking words I had heard her read aloud at home. Our home now.

It confused me because the men called her by a name I had not heard before, and then all action stopped on command. She was called a different name by the same people and then the party began all over again, on command. In my fascination with all the unfamiliar activity, I must have buzzed a little and flitted from object to object without exactly paying attention to where I was going.

Camera Operator: (in a loud voice) "There's a fly on the set. Get him out!"

"Uh oh, spotted again," I thought.

Immediately, the sloppily dressed men and women surrounding the party scene located me and attacked me with rolled-up newspapers, towels, wadded-up shirts, and anything that could be used as a weapon. I flew straight up to the beams that held the lights, but there were people there as well.

Lighting Grip: "He's up here."

I knew I was in big trouble again, so when the door to the room opened to let someone in, I raced out. Unlike the executioners on the sound stage, no one in the hallway paid any attention to me, and I could linger there waiting for Barbara to finish what she was doing.

Good thing, too. I was exhausted, scared, and resolved never to venture into a room like the last one, where flies were not welcome. But for my reflexes, a full 200-Hertz faster than the human eye can react, I would have been a spot on the wall. That's my edge.

Why do people hate flies so much? Their first instinct is to kill them instantly. People seem to be annoyed much of the time, and not just with flies. It's just that we can't fight back. We make an easy target, and nobody cares much when another fly bites the dust.

Flies get no respect, not like tarantulas or scorpions, which can do some damage with their bites, stingers, and the poison they carry. Bees are respected because they have stingers and they can fight back.

I wouldn't mind plunging a stinger into some aggressive fool waving the Sunday paper at me just because I interrupted his reading of the comic section. I might like to become a bee. A pretty multicolored bee, not the drab brown coloration of the average fly. I suppose that makes me a wannabee.

While I was thinking this, Barbara, still in costume, burst from the party set, raced down the hallway, and exited the building. I followed behind, a little too slow and cautious, having been nearly killed in the last two rooms I visited.

Barbara unlocked the car with her remote and slid in. An older man, who was waiting beside the car in the parking lot smoking a cigar, got in, and they were off. I knew she would be leaving, but I was still in shock. Suddenly, I was left on my own in the parking lot with no food, no protection, and no idea of what to do. Being alone in the world outside of the house was tougher than I had imagined.

Chapter 6
Flies and Dogs

I flew around aimlessly until I spotted a dumpster where several flies were hard at work, mining food from yesterday's garbage. I settled on a telephone pole where I had a clear view of the dumpster, the flies, and a nearby park where people walked their dogs. I flew down for a closer look.

Those house flies were a scruffy lot; hairy, scarred, and none too friendly. Fruit flies are more refined. I approached cautiously, looking for a little companionship and maybe some food. Flies don't eat much at every meal, they have to eat continuously to stay alive. It's a matter of first things first, so the resident flies were busy and not prone to being sociable.

Once inside the dumpster, a manic group of flies had settled on half a bagel with a few ragged edges of lox and not one of them was inclined to give an inch to a newcomer. My stomach turned at the prospect of eating this filthy trash.

I had become accustomed to eating fresh food from a clean plate at home. I buzzed back up to the edge of the dumpster, where a really unattractive female housefly was perched. She gave me the signs and odors that she was ready for me to have sex with her to fertilize her eggs. I blew off this fly, and she pursued me, even taunting me for not responding. I told her I had a headache. I yearned to be home in Malibu.

Flies don't have headaches. I could have told her that I was too old for her, having by far outlived my thirty-day lifespan, but I doubted she would understand that either.

While I processed this dilemma, the female housefly spotted a load of dog excrement by the side of the dumpster and flew down to investigate. Typical housefly behavior. Fruit flies are not so prone to the disgusting conduct of house flies.

Houseflies hang out in dead carcasses, dumpsters, sewer systems, and animal excrement. They are the real spreaders of disease, not us fruit flies. There was no way I considered going along with this program, but it did make me think about why people hate flies. If this is what flies are attracted to, then I want no part of it.

I knew that I needed to wait for Barbara to return, so I could not go too far from the place where she parked her car. I had seen the park, which was not far from the CBS building, and I made my way there, looking for a better class of food and company.

The park was mostly empty, but a few people were walking their dogs. I had seen them on the beach in Malibu, and I can't say I was wild about these creatures. They deposit their excrement at random, and nobody pays much attention to it. Flies and other dogs sniff around it endlessly, and that doesn't make a good impression on me.

Dogs are a lot like flies, in that they always pursue the worst of the garbage to be found in trash cans, dumpsters, and litter. They're more aggressive because of their size and strength. Even the well-groomed dogs, who fawn and slobber over their masters and seem so well-behaved on their leashes, wearing dainty sweaters, vests, booties, and collars, are ungovernable monsters.

They lick the master's face, and then a second later, jam their noses up another dog's butt, or into a pile of shit. I don't see what makes people so crazy about these animals, why they let them sleep on their beds, watch television on their couches, pamper them with expensive food, and generally make fools of themselves trying to please them.

The dogs are welcome in every room in the house, even in the kitchen where food is everywhere. It's not unusual for them to sit under a table, or next to it while the family is eating, and be hand-fed choice morsels of food I would die for.

These befuddled dog lovers hate the insects that the dog carries around on its body, and believe me dogs have tons of insects on them all the time. I have flown around a few of these beasts in Malibu, watching the insects on their backs and private parts dance feverishly about, like jumping beans.

Do these dedicated pet owners realize that dogs are like mobile insect hotels? They don't begin to react until they learn that the dog has fleas. Then they sprinkle some benign expensive but ineffectual powder on the pooch instead of paying attention to those black insects that burrow into the dog's skin. They would have to set the dog on fire to get rid of the fleas if they knew the truth.

When I flew in front of these dogs, their breath nearly melted my wings. They fart continuously, polluting the air that their masters breathe. And the barking; that guttural, harsh, meaningless sound they give off - like a wartime air raid blast or a foghorn tornado warning. Any rational person would be irritated, but dog lovers seem to think it's cute or even has meaning.

The buzzing of a fly, by comparison, is a love song, yet it drives people nuts. The barking, at worst, gets a pat on the head with a soothing warning to calm down and a doggie biscuit to make the dumb brute happy. The fly doesn't get a warning, he earns a crushing blow that terminates his life.

This is so unjust. A well-fed fly would make a much better pet.

Chapter 7
A Brutal Accident

I had spent enough time watching dogs and evading houseflies. Since flies have no sense of time, I was unaware of how much time had elapsed since Barbara drove away. I had to wait where I could see her return, and hope that I could find my way back into her car when she returned home. I migrated back to the CBS parking lot to a shady tree, overlooking the entry gate and the city street.

Below me were several vehicles parked one behind the other on the quiet street, devoid of traffic at the moment. I had a good view of the car closest to the gate, a bright red convertible sports car with the top down, parked ahead of an old, gray pickup truck.

The occupant of the sports car was a young, good-looking man consumed with the act of combing his thick black hair, which gleamed in the bright afternoon sun. His hand, which held the comb, was adorned with a large red signet ring that caught the light and attracted my attention.

The grooming session ended when the man checked his rear mirror, to determine if his hair was combed in a manner that he deemed suitable. He then started the engine, which emitted a high-volume roar that brought a smile to the driver's face and which he seemed in no hurry to end. Perhaps the engine's power spoke to him of adventure and excitement. The engine idled while he pulled out his cell phone, punched in some numbers, and spoke briefly to the person who answered.

While the sports car continued to growl menacingly, another person, a dark-complected man, approached and entered the beat-up gray pickup truck parked behind the red sports car. He was, by far, the largest man I had ever seen.

Of course, all people looked like giants to me because of my size, or lack thereof, but this man looked like a moving mountain. His arms were the size of a normal man's legs, and his legs looked like tree trunks. He held a cup of coffee and a chocolate muffin, whose scent I could almost taste, in his gigantic hand as he dawdled in the driver's seat of the truck sipping his coffee.

I was drawn by the scent of the muffin off the tree as if I were magnetized. I had not eaten much in the CBS building before the series of unprovoked attempts on my life. The windows of the pickup truck were open, and the prospect of even a few crumbs was irresistible. Both drivers were motionless, the sports car guy on his cell phone, the engine still roaring, the giant with his coffee, and the muffin I coveted.

My strategy was to zip through the window and be gone before either vehicle moved. Not so easy, since flies don't have teeth and must linger over a morsel to suck and digest the tiniest bit of nutrients. It didn't matter. I chose nutrition over safety and flew down to the truck, landing momentarily at the open passenger side window.

Immediately, the engine noise of the sports car gave way to the jarring sounds of a metal vs. metal collision. The sports car exploded backward into the front of the truck like a guided missile. Glass shattered. Tires squealed. Then dead silence. The driver of the sports car failed to grasp that his transmission was in reverse, having been more interested in his hair and cell phone use.

The crash jolted me off the window as if jerked by an invisible hand. I barely avoided the tsunami of hot coffee that reared up from the plastic cup that had been jolted from the giant's hand.

He was not so lucky, as he lurched back and then snapped forward violently against the steering wheel and then the windshield. He was briefly unconscious, then began to move his head and arms over the wheel, a cut over his eye leaking blood down his cheek and onto his shirt. I wasn't certain that he was human until then, but the blood confirmed his membership in the human species.

Both cars and both people were still and silent for what seemed like a long time.

Finally, the pretty boy driver, who initiated the accident, got out of his car and surveyed the damage. He looked in all directions, presumably to determine if anyone had seen the accident. That would be me, an insignificant insect with twelve thousand lens eyes that allowed me to see in every direction. Of course, he ignored me. He could not ignore the cracked windshield and the crumpled hood and bumper of the truck. He came closer to the wounded vehicle and peered into the open driver's side window at the injured, unconscious giant.

Mr. Pretty Boy must have realized that he had collided with a rare and unusual being. The injured man's head nearly filled up the driver's side window. He wore a tweed wool cap with a short front bill that had fallen onto his lap during the accident. He was bald except for a monk's fringe of dark hair, an older man, to my surprise.

Muttered sentence fragments were emerging from the distressed man, half-conscious mumblings from a voice as deep as he was large. His tone was angry. I wasn't so happy myself. I could not locate even a fragment of the muffin that I desperately needed.

The victim of the accident was struggling toward consciousness, a word escaping from his mouth that I had heard earlier in the day directed at me.

Victim: "Mufu, mufu."

Even muffled and slurred it conveyed a menace to the neatly combed cause of the accident. He was holding a business card, and was about to leave it on the dashboard with his information. He glanced at the card, then back at the giant, and stuck the card into his pants pocket as he rushed back to his car. He leaped into the shiny red leather bucket seat of his car, restarted the engine, and raced away from the damaged pickup and its stunned occupant. He was gone without a backward glance.

I spotted what Barbara calls a vanity license place, undamaged from the crash. Through the windshield, I saw the plate but didn't know what it meant. I couldn't read, but I memorized the shapes should I ever see the car again. It looked like $RES, as the car pulled away.

I found a little of the chocolate muffin on the passenger seat that I had missed at first, and got what I could out of it. I managed enough to keep me going before the big man came to his senses. He shook his damaged head, arose, and left the inside of the vehicle to inspect the damage outside. He was shaky and moved like Barbara's ex-boyfriend, Adam, when he had too much to drink.

The injured man searched for a witness, his anger growing with the realization of what had happened. I wanted to tell him what happened, but lacking the gift of speech, I could not. When he re-entered his vehicle, he observed me lingering on the dashboard by the passenger window. He pounded the steering wheel with his fist in frustration.

Victim: (growling in my direction) "Only a fuckin' fly."

He didn't attempt to swat or strike me.

Victim: "Not one damn witness. That mother fuckin' honkey coulda killed me and gotten away with it. I bet you saw the whole damn thing."

He glared at me as if he could force me to talk. I would gladly have done so, sad that I could not communicate directly with any human. If I could talk, then I could have made use of my supernatural ability to think. If I could only do that, I would be connected to the world around me, not just a lonely freak.

Of course, humans would not be happy to know that a virtually invisible presence with this ability was lurking about. They already despised flies and other insects. I wanted to tell them that insects existed long before these bipeds took over the earth. Humans are just newcomers compared to insects.

The man lost interest in me as he mopped the blood from his face with a piece of cloth, delivered a final blow to the steering wheel, and then pulled himself together. I retreated to the tree, where I watched the pickup pull slowly away, the front bumper scraping the ground. I was tempted to go with him in his truck, thinking that he might be the one person I could connect with.

He was the first person, besides Barbara, who looked at me without disdain or hatred. But I didn't. I was fixed on my plan to return to Malibu and the sweet life with Barbara, if I could find her.

When I resumed my vigil in the tree above the entry gate, there was her metal banana parked in the lot. She was saying goodbye to her agent. He left the car puffing on his cigar, with the window open so that he would not offend his client by stinking up her car.

Like a speeding bullet, I was in that car, rooting around on the carpet for some food. My wings were nearly set on fire by a smoldering ash from the cigar that blew in from the outdoors. Barbara's human friends had the most disgusting habits. I couldn't wait to get home and put this hectic, frightening day behind me.

Chapter 8
A Day at the Races

The next morning, she slept late, showered, dressed casually, and then told me what we were about to do. I hovered over her bedroom dresser while she dressed and talked to me.

Barbara: "We are going to the race track today. My daddy used to take me to the horse races in Texas. He always lost betting on the horses. When the day was done, he'd say to me, 'If I was a fly on the wall in the jockey room, I'd know who won every race, and you and I would be rich today.'

When I saw that picture of the horse and jockey in the magazine, I remembered me and my daddy at the races. You won't be my daddy. You will be the fly on the wall in the jockeys' room.

"You will go into the room where the jockeys get dressed before they ride in a race. You will listen to what the jockeys say about the upcoming race, and which horse they think has the best chance to win. You will then fly back to me before the race begins, and I will read to you the names of the horses from the racing form."

"When you hear either the name or the number of the horse that the jockeys picked to win, you will buzz like crazy. Then I will point to the name of the horse on the racing form, and read you the name and number; you will land on the form next to my finger, to make sure we have it right."

"I've arranged a private box for us so nobody will see what we're doing. Everyone at the track is busy with their bets, and we should not draw any attention. There are also lots of flies on the track and lots of people and noise. No one should even notice you in my box, or the jockey's room."

"All you have to do is listen and bring back the information. That's what a fly on the wall is supposed to do, overhear gossip. We are just going to take it one step further."

When we arrived at the track, Barbara asked one of the maintenance men where the jockey's room was located, and she explained to me how I should find it. I made my way into the room, along with some horseflies who seemed right at home, so I was just another fly buzzing around. The men were all short but very fit.

One group of men spoke Spanish, which I could not understand, so I sought out the English speakers, hoping they would talk about the first race of the day.

Jockey one: "I got the number two horse. He's the favorite. He hates this wet track. We might as well not leave the barn."

Jockey two: (wearing different colored silks) "My horse is a worthless nag. I'm only riding to do his trainer a favor."

Jockey one: "So, who do you like in this?"

Jockey three: "I like the five horse. He's had some workouts on muddy tracks, and his times are good. It's a short race, six furlongs, so that helps him."

The group nodded in agreement. There was more talk about weight assignments and moving up and down in classifications, but I'd heard enough.

I flew out of the room and checked out the horses being walked around the show ring before the race. The five horse wasn't much to look at. He was smaller than his competition, and he was docile, even relaxed, compared to the others who strutted about, tossed their heads imperiously, kicked up their heels, and generally behaved as if they were superior creatures entitled to all the attention they were getting. The favorites reminded me of those "executives" in the CBS commissary. They were almost as pretty as the horses, and half as smart.

I wasn't sure that number five was the right choice. What does a fly know about horse racing? I only knew that this was a test for me, and I wanted to be right, or I could be out on the street to fend for myself. This one moment was in the hands of the gods - another line I heard from a television series. I think it means only the supernatural, the God humans always turn to, can bend things your way. It isn't much to rely on, from what I've seen.

Their God isn't much interested in flies. Lacking a vocabulary, a fly can't speak or think a prayer. Still, if you want something desperately, a human prayer seems to be an alternative when everything else fails. I haven't found the right time to pray. Perhaps I need some instruction, but that would have to come with some religious guidance, and I don't know which religion would suit a mutant fly."

"I would need a place to pray, like a church building with a serious, reverent setting. Of course, I would not be welcome in a church. I would be a disturbance, the same as I was on the movie set. I suppose I could pray in my broom closet, which doesn't seem sufficiently dignified to hold God's ear. And what would I pray for anyway, entry to an afterlife? This begs the question; are there flies in heaven?

Back in our private box, Barbara read off the names and numbers of the horses in the first race. The five horse, Flight Plan, was pointed out to me and I landed alongside Barbara's index finger.

Barbara: "Flight Plan, number five. Are you absolutely sure that's the one?"

I buzzed twice, as loud as I could. We went through this three times before she nodded, grabbed her purse, and headed for the betting windows. I learned when she came back that Flight Plan was a 20-1 long shot and had not run lately because of an injury. She informed me that she had made a $200 bet on Flight Plan to win. Now I was praying for the right result to save my sorry ass. There would be more time as the race still had not been run.

I tried harder to silently pray, but how could a silent prayer to an unknown, unfamiliar, mystical, and distant entity do anything to help me? I concluded that I could pray all day from sunrise to sunset, and the race would be won by the fastest horse ridden by the best jockey.

The race itself didn't take long. It was more of a sprint than a marathon. Barbara was on her feet and screaming the second the horses left the gate.

About halfway through the race, Flight Plan surged to the front and stayed there, kicking up clods of mud into the faces of his betters. Barbara raced to the cashier's window nearly as fast as the horses on the track. I looked over her shoulder as she turned in her ticket, and the man at the cashier's window counted out a huge wad of bills.

Barbara: (screaming) "$4,000!"

Had my prayers been answered? Probably not. The jockeys knew the answer, not me and not the inscrutable deity of the humans.

Heads turned as one in the line of bettors at the windows. Most of them were buying tickets with their social security checks for the next race.

Mutual clerk: "Pretty nice wager. If you look down the hallway to the end of the room, there's an IRS office, where they will take some of this money and deduct it for withholding taxes. I am instructed to direct you there. But don't worry, it won't be that much, you're still a big winner."

Barbara gave him her biggest smile, and he seemed genuinely pleased for her. Not a bad quality to have. You win, you get money, you smile and everybody loves you. I think this has a lot to do with Barbara's beauty. It wouldn't be this way for most humans.

We returned to her box, where she already had out her racing form. She sent me back to the jockey's room, but this time I overheard no conversation was of any use. In our box, I wanted to shake my head, but instead, all I could do was park myself on the bottom of the page of the racing form. She pointed again at each horse listed on the form and when I didn't alight next to her finger, she got the message.

Barbara: "Buzz three times if you heard nothing about this race."

I did so, and she knew I was not holding out on her.

Barbara: "So, our plan isn't perfect, but it's damn good."

She was caressing the bundle of cash from the first race, still substantial after the IRS took withholding. Barbara was not yet earning the kind of money she would in the future when this amount would seem trivial.

Barbara: "You did just fine, a good day's work. I don't want to risk bad bets in the last seven races. That's what my father would have done. He'd stay here dripping wet in the rain and bet every race until he ran out of money."

That was fine with me because the rain was still coming down and I was wet and tired. You don't see many flies when it rains, with good reason. My wet wings felt like lead weights and I could barely make it to the car. But I knew I had done my job and a career had just begun.

I had a purpose in life and a patron to protect me. I was Barbara's secret weapon, capable of passing information that made money for her.

I saw no moral violation and awaited my next assignment, assuming that one would be coming for me soon. Against my better judgment, I indulged in a silent prayer asking God, or whoever was aware of my prayer, to send me more information like number five, Flight Plan.

Pretty selfish, I thought to myself. God must have more important requests to ponder.

Chapter 9
The Neighbors

Barbara, in our new phase, treated me like a long-lost prince. I had my sleeping quarters in the pantry, close to the kitchen, where fruit and other delicacies were now left out for me. No more sharing with other people or greedy insects. I was allowed to follow her out for her walks and runs on the beach. It was exercise for me as well. We watched television and streamed shows and videos from social media together.

She had long ago discontinued her relationship with Adam, but closed the door on me to keep me out of the bedroom and bathroom, although she was nice enough to apologize for this change. Actually, it did hurt my feelings. What a surprise. Flies have feelings.

I realized that before we communicated, I was suffering from severe stress. I was merely an unwelcome guest in a comfortable place. I had no life plan, just a day-to-day existence. Lacking a real identity, I had no idea how to behave around people or other flies. I was incapable of sustaining a relationship due to my own insecurity and yet I blamed my circumstances for this condition.

Like all flies, I was jittery and nervous to a fault, obsessed with my degraded physical and emotional condition. I had no pride in being a flying insect.

All that changed when I discovered my ability to observe and communicate. I was no longer embarrassed by my appearance, which had changed for the better. I took on a rich, dark color; my legs acquired a pleasing shape; my body filled out, my wings expanded, and my eyes were sharper and less red. Female flies were drawn to me, but I had no interest and turned them away. I suppose they saw in me the alpha male, fully developed, eager to fertilize and propagate my species. It was their fantasy, not mine.

I even noticed that some people, not all, no longer seemed repulsed or irritated by my presence. On occasion, I could linger without fear. Even my buzzing took on a deeper, richer, more musical sound. I was becoming a fully realized fly. I no longer speculated about becoming a bee, when I discovered that male bees only live to serve the Queen and afterward, are murdered by the Queen's female helpers. Flies really are more civilized.

However, I learned from watching bees that they communicate with one another by dancing. Primarily, they tell one another where the food can be located. Flies, on the other hand, are capitalists; every fly for itself.

I saw communication with Barbara as my first step on the evolutionary ladder, perhaps the beginning of a new order for my species. I didn't know how Barbara saw this development, whether it went beyond funneling information to her. Simply put, it would have to play out on its own. There are no models, books, films, or self-proclaimed experts that provide instructions for inter-species communication.

Since we were still in the experimentation stage, Barbara would generate ideas and tell me to execute them. Not everything worked, and we were hard-pressed at times to communicate accurately. Frustration was not uncommon.

There was the time she sent me next door to report on her neighbors, a middle-aged couple who lived in an expansive, glass-dominated home adjoining the beach. It was no trouble getting into the house to observe them. Seems like people in Malibu all leave their windows open.

I learned that Frank was a former military officer who became an insurance executive upon retirement from the army. I wasn't sure what insurance meant when I started hanging around their house, but I got the idea after a while. Insurance, according to Frank, the husband, meant taking money from people who were afraid that something bad might happen to them, and if something bad did happen, then the insurance company was supposed to pay for the loss to the person who was afraid to begin with, and suffered loss or damage.

There were many variations on this theme, like car accidents, robbery, fire, flood, earthquake, and heart attacks; the list of things to insure against was endless.

The insurance company kept the money if nothing bad happened. This seemed like a really good deal, almost too good to be true. If something negative did happen, the insurance company would find reasons not to pay. If they paid, it would only be a small amount of the damage or loss. Frank, managed many people called "adjusters," who were no more than lowly clerks sent by him to supposedly "investigate" incidents and report to Frank. By design, the investigations were solely for the benefit of the insurance company.

Frank was paid big money to tell people what they would be paid, which was often less than what they were entitled to. Frank called this good business. He didn't do any investigation himself; he just said no to every claim made. I could tell from his phone conversation that he based his judgments on a deeply held belief that all the complaints and claims were exaggerated, and that the people who made the claims were liars and fakers.

He held a lot of stock in the company and much of his conversation had to do with fluctuations in the market price which showed up in the business section of the newspaper he read. Most days, Frank paid little attention to the front page, but went directly to the financial section. He was locked in to the point that he ignored everyone and everything while he read the quotes and articles.

Over time, I edged closer to the paper and peered over Frank's shoulder as he zeroed in on the stock. He was so intent on the daily volume, the 200-day moving average, and the analyst articles, that I could have been a buzzard with a ten-foot wing span and he would never have noticed me.

Frank talked endlessly on the phone to someone he called his broker. If the stock was up, he was pleased, and if it was down, he was grouchy and unpleasant, to his broker, to his underlings, but mainly to his wife, Ethel.

Ethel didn't have much to do around the house except straighten up after Frank. She had a woman come in to clean up every other day. She went shopping for food but never cooked or prepared a meal herself. She shopped for clothes that didn't look anything like the clothes Barbara wore. All her clothes were either black, grey, or brown, dull and shapeless. Frank wasn't dressed much better. He always wore a baggy suit and colorless tie on every occasion. I thought he might even sleep in his suit.

She read magazines, one of which had a story about Barbara in it. She even gossiped about Barbara on the phone to her friends. She bragged to one woman about living next to a movie star and then to another she called Barbara trashy. She slept late while Frank went to work.

They went out for dinner a lot and Ethel liked to dress up and wear her jewelry to go with her boring clothing. At night, she watched television shows with laugh tracks, spent a lot of time in her bathroom, and rarely had sex with Frank. Theirs was not the most entertaining household, but Barbara kept sending me back hoping that I could find something about Frank and Ethel that would be useful to her. I could not think of much; their conversations ran to the following:

Frank or Ethel: "What did you do today?"
or

Ethel or Frank: "How was work today?",
or

Frank or Ethel: "Where should we have dinner tonight?"

They never went out on the beach but complained when other people put up umbrellas in front of their house, or when dogs and children made noise. Frank traveled now and then to insurance conferences and seminars on the corporate plane with other company executives, always without his wife.

One day, Frank came home smiling and unusually cheerful. He told Ethel to dress up, they were going out to celebrate. His company was about to acquire another company, one even bigger and richer than his own, and he knew the price of his stock would double. It was the little fish eating the big fish.

This was the information I was waiting for and when I returned to my place, I landed and danced on the newspaper for Barbara. She picked up the paper and went through it page by page.

When she came to the financial page, I buzzed repeatedly, and she dropped the rest of the paper. I flew down and landed on the symbol for Frank's insurance company, which I had seen so often from my vantage point over Frank's shoulder.

Barbara: "Should I buy or sell? One buzz for buy, two buzzes for sell.

I gave her my deepest musical buzz to buy. To make sure we had it right, she repeated this several times. She even pointed out other symbols on the same page and when I kept returning to the same symbol for Frank's company, she felt confident that the information concerned just that one stock. Barbara got on the phone with her broker the next morning and told him to buy 1000 shares at $25 a share. Within three weeks the stock had risen to $50 per share, and Barbara had doubled her money. Her broker demanded to know how she decided on this stock.

He never learned it came from a fly on the wall. He would never learn this fact.

I was the hero of this little drama, and it only whetted Barbara's appetite for more financial adventures with me as the focal point. We were both gaining confidence.

Frank and Ethel made hundreds of thousands on this stock, but nothing much changed for them. Frank still came home grouchy from his office. Ethel still shopped and talked on the phone. They bought a new car that looked exactly like the old one. They had perfunctory sex every so often and dinner out every few nights. They watched the same television shows, and read the same papers and the same magazines. I stopped coming to their house, and they never noticed.

Chapter 10
A Vacation

Back at home, Barbara wanted to reward me, but was hard-pressed to find the right thing. Flies don't drive new cars, wear jewelry, sport expensive clothes, handmade Italian shoes, or drink Dom Perignon.

She could hardly give me a lavish party and invite all of her famous and nearly famous friends. She would be locked up in a mental ward for throwing a party for her fly.

I did think some tasteful jewelry might be nice, a diamond discreetly placed under my stomach so as not to attract too much attention, but that could be painful. I couldn't get a tattoo or even a small piercing, it would likely kill me. Finally, we decided to take a trip to Las Vegas, give me a change of scenery, and possibly find another way to enrich ourselves.

Barbara: "Let's just follow the money."

She booked us into a suite at the Bellagio Hotel and ordered baskets of fresh fruit to be delivered upon our arrival. We drove in her flashy Mercedes, top-up, so I would not be blown away to languish out my existence in Victorville or Barstow. They didn't lack for flies in those towns, with temperatures in the hundreds and trash strewn all over the roads and gutters.

This could have been my short little life but for the intervention of a kind fate. Not for me, scrabbling in the dust, fighting over morsels in scuzzy garbage cans and dumpsters. I could be fertilizing eggs from females and fathering creatures in whom I had no interest. It made me humble to realize the position in life I had achieved in a relatively short time, and it fired my ambition to go even further.

My destiny was linked to Barbara, the only person I could communicate with. Would she use me? Would I influence her in the pursuit of my goals? Come to think of it, I lacked clear goals, and I had no idea what Barbara's goals were, beyond making some easy money. But what is money to a fly?

Nothing material means anything to a fly, except for food, so a fly can't be bought, bribed, blackmailed, or busted. That's a lot more than can be said for people. Flies exist in a moral vacuum, yet they are blameless to a fault.

And that saying people use, "He wouldn't hurt a fly," is nonsense. A fly is always fair game. The phrase should be reversed, as in, "A fly would never hurt anyone." Such were my thoughts as the dreary desert scenery scrolled by on the road to Las Vegas.

Things were not so easy in Las Vegas. At night the neon lights, blinking, flashing, moving into images of girls, gamblers, and shows, had me off balance. Inside the casinos, the roar of slot machines, hysterical gamblers, cell phones, and people shouting for drinks or attention, distracted me from listening at my normal level.

I could not find a comfort level except in our suite, but Barbara didn't want to stay there alone. She wanted action for herself, and she wanted me to eavesdrop on the card dealers, the surveillance and security staff, backstage at the shows, and anything she thought would provide information. I tried but had no luck.

Nobody paid any attention to me, which under normal circumstances would be fine. I could have been on fire, a flaming, dive-bombing insect, and no one would have been the wiser in this manic world of gamblers, tourists, gawkers, and hustlers.

Maybe I had been around people too long, so I did what most seem to do when discouraged or defeated. I went to a bar in the hotel. At least I had company there; men and women slumped over their drinks, licking their wounds, pouring down cheap liquor at expensive prices to dilute their sorrows. It was darker and quieter than on the casino floor. For once I could comfortably eavesdrop, which now seemed to be my purpose in life.

Two expensively dressed men in their fifties, tanned but looking tired, with dark circles under their eyes, seemed to be sharing some life truths with one another at the bar. I listened in from my vantage point on the back of a nearby bar stool.

Man one: "My wife loves it here, so we come from Chicago twice a year."

Man two: "We come from Jersey."

Man one: "Are you connected out here?"

Man two: "You could say that. How about you?"

Man one: "I know just enough people and manage to drop enough money at the tables to get comped."

Man two: "They got a sweet operation here. Give away the hotel rooms, and people can't lose their money fast enough. Then the hotels double up on the food, the wine, the spa, the shopping, and the shows. Pretty smart for a bunch of dumb wops from Jersey."

Man one: "You watch the Sopranos? That's what you sound like."

Man two: "I love that show, they got it right."

Man one: "I was never sure. I thought it was made up. You know, middle-class guys busting up other guys for gambling debts, running hookers, fixing ball games, then arguing with their wives and kids at the dinner table about how much money the wife spends at the mall."

Man two: "Everyone's got a job to do."

There was a huge television screen above the bar, and a football game was in progress. Both men glanced up at the screen periodically as they spoke and drank. They were doing a lot of the latter and their friendship seemed to expand with each round of doubles.

Man one: "You a big sports fan? People in Chicago are nuts about Pro sports. The Bears, the Bulls, the Blackhawks. Me too."

Man two: "Yeah, I love the Giants and the Knicks too. I bet the basketball but not the football. With five guys on the floor, one guy hurt or out makes a big difference in the odds."

Man one: "I don't know. In football, if you have a great quarterback, you always win, and if he goes down, you can pretty much figure out what will happen to his team."

Man two: "It's not always about winning or losing, it's the spread. I bet the basketball since I happen to know about a ref in the NBA you can count on to make the spread."

Man one: "You're kidding me. A fixed ref in the NBA?"

Man two: "Listen to me, if it's got two legs and you can talk to it, anything can be fixed. I don't care if it's a jockey, a politician, a judge, or a football player. They have gambling debts, mortgages, mistresses, or boyfriends to pay off and no way to get it. Some are greedy, some are desperate; there's always a reason."

Man one: "So who wins this ballgame, the one we're looking at, the Saints or the Raiders?"

Man two: "Shit, I don't know, it doesn't happen every day, or at least I don't know about every game."

Man one: "Too bad."

Man two: "Tell you what. You and your wife meet us for dinner tonight, and I'll give you a little tip. My treat. If you win, the next one is your treat, and we'll go the whole hog on your ticket."

Man one: "You're on, buddy. Bartender, two more doubles here."

I found Barbara and buzzed around her while she received the fawning admiration of several hotel employees and guests. They had plans for her to be introduced at their theater, a dinner for her at the hotel's gourmet restaurant, golf lessons, and a shopping spree at the hotel shops, with photographers recording every moment as she tried on clothing, jewelry, shoes and whatever else looked good to her.

When we returned to our suite, it was now crowded with flowers, fruit baskets, candy, and champagne, I landed on a newspaper, buzzing at max volume until I earned Barbara's attention.

She knew to thumb through it until I landed on the item of interest. This time, when she got to the sports section, I settled on a picture of large black men leaping in the air and stayed on it.

She questioned me but I could not provide answers. Without the power of speech, we played an endless guessing game, often resulting in mutual frustration.

All she could make out was that I was somehow interested in basketball and we had to leave it there, while she sampled the goodies left in the room by management and various admirers.

Later, she bathed, talked on the phone, and primped and dressed for dinner. Upon entering the restaurant, I saw the two guys from the bar seated with their wives at one of the better tables.

I flew over the table and Barbara grasped my intention. She asked the maître de for a table near them, and he obliged seeing as Barbara was dining with the hotel manager. She smiled at the two couples as she was seated, and it had an electric effect on the women as well as the men. The whispering began as soon as she turned her attention elsewhere.

Woman one: "My god, she is gorgeous, even prettier than on screen. I saw her on Y and R not long ago. She stole the show."

Man two: "Did you see that smile? She could light up the entire Midwest."

Woman two: "I just love Vegas. You never see the stars in Jersey."

Man two: "You got "Soprano" look-a-likes."

I landed on the edge of their table and lingered there on and off through dinner. They were all smiles talking about Barbara, and with the wine and drinks flowing they paid scant attention to their food. After the second bottle of wine and the third round of drinks, the guy from Jersey leaned over to his friend. We were nearly face-to-face as he whispered in his ear.

Man two: "Tomorrow night. The Celtics and the Bucks. The Celtics will lose, but they will make the spread. Get down on it at the Sportsbook here, and don't be shy about it."

The guy from Chicago just nodded and proposed a toast to his new friends, suggesting another dinner for the two happy couples. I could tell from his body language that he wanted to jump up right now and run to make his bet, but he held his place until the meal was finished.

Meanwhile, Barbara was charming the pants off the hotel manager, a trim, nice-looking man in his early fifties with a shaven head and a diamond earring in one ear. She hardly glanced at me as I snatched a few bites of the leftover crème brûlée.

Once again, I forgot that flies are always vulnerable and the Latino busboy just missed me with a rolled-up napkin. Barbara saw this happen and rose suddenly out of her seat, an anguished look on her lovely face.

Hotel Manager: "Is something wrong?"

Seeing that I had survived she composed herself and sat back down.

Barbara: "Nothing, it's nothing at all."

She did look genuinely concerned, even frightened. It made me feel like she cared about me. We retreated from the restaurant together and made a brief stop at a blackjack table, where Barbara was nearly mobbed by other gamblers and hangers-on. She might have stayed longer, but I kept flying toward the exit, and she picked up on my desire to get down to the business of reporting my information.

I jumped on the open sports page of the newspaper back in our suite. There were no articles or photographs related to the Celtics-Bucks game, but I managed to find a Celtics logo on the slate of upcoming games. Barbara grasped my interest. Something was going on specific to that team. I had to convey to her that any bet must take into account the point spread.

She was asking me which team to bet on, the Celtics or the Bucks. I answered no to both questions, and she was puzzled. I then persuaded her by body language to open up the hotel guide, which described the various gambling choices, and landed on the Sports Book entry. She got the point that the bet had something to do with the Sports Book, so we left the room again and went downstairs to the Sports Book.

The basketball and football games were listed individually on a large computerized board with the point spread and the odds shown for each contest. I flew to the Celtics-Bucks game and then flew back and forth between the game listing and the point spread. Barbara asked a savvy-looking male bettor what was meant by the point spread and of course, the guy was delighted to have her attention.

He explained the point spread, taking as much time as possible, throwing in random observations about Vegas, in general. He flattered Barbara at every opportunity while holding himself out as the foremost betting expert in North America.

Barbara played along beautifully, until she was certain that she understood the concept and grasped the fact that I wanted her to take the Celtics to make the spread. Mr. Know-it-all disagreed.

Mr. Know it all: "The Celtics are terrible this year. They have no talent to speak of, their best player is injured and not up to par, their management is dysfunctional and they're playing on the road. The fans and the refs are a big factor for a team on the road, and so is the travel and rest factor. I don't know where they stay in Milwaukee, but wherever that is, it won't satisfy all the young, over-paid millionaires who are used to the top level of hotels and luxury. They probably can't get the service, the drugs, or the caliber of girls they want. They're very likely complaining right now about going to dull, drab Milwaukee where the strip clubs can't compete with New York and LA."

Barbara nodded her agreement, went to the betting station, and promptly took the Celtics to make the spread with three thousand dollars at nine to two odds. Later she went on the internet to get information on the Celtics and discovered that Mr. Know-it-all had essentially been correct in his analysis. The Bucks were on a five-game winning streak, and leading their division. Naturally, she questioned my information, but all I could do was remain mute, handicapped as I was.

The Sports Book called to question Barbara's sizeable bet because the limit was $1,000. She had paid cash, and with her influence at the hotel had no trouble retaining the bet. She also explained to the Book that she was a lifetime Celtics fan and proceeded to impress the Book with her encyclopedic knowledge of Celtics past and present, a history of the Boston Gardens and the Fleet Center, Red Auerbach's influence on the present NBA, and the type of cigar he lit when victory was assured.

It's truly amazing how twenty minutes on the internet can make anyone with a good memory an expert on any given subject. Her bet was approved.

The next morning, I trailed behind Barbara as she headed out to a private VIP swimming pool. We left our suite to walk through the main hallway that led through the casino, and then outdoors. Strutting down the corridor was none other than our neighbor Frank, dressed in a trendy golf outfit in bright maroon pants and a matching golf shirt with a pretty Asian girl, half his age, on his arm. He gesticulated with his free arm, no doubt something to do with his golf game. For a moment I thought he might be waving hello to me.

He traipsed right past us, oblivious to the fact that I had spotted him living a secret life. He was fortunate I was a mute and had nobody, except Ethel, to report Frank's treachery. Had I been more experienced in the turns and twists of human behavior, I would not have been so shocked. No wonder Frank viewed most insurance claimants as liars and fakes. He was one of them.

That same night the Celtics-Bucks game was televised, along with all the other NBA games in the Sports Book lounge. Barbara was caught up in the action as the Bucks hammered the Celtics throughout the first half of play. I received some very dirty looks at halftime, but none as dirty as the Chicago businessman was throwing at his New Jersey pal. Barbara was indirectly threatening me with a rolled-up magazine, which she slapped on the table from time to time, glancing in my direction.

The Celtics didn't rally until the fourth quarter, when they cut a fifteen-point deficit to ten mid-way through the quarter. The spread was six needed to win the bet, meaning that Barbara would lose her bet if the game ended in a Buck's win by anything more than six points.

In the quarter, the score went up and down, the Bucks up by ten, then up eight. For what seemed a half hour (time outs, free throws, lots of fouls) the score stayed at plus seven for the Bucks, which would mean good money down the drain for Barbara, and a full-fledged disaster for the Chicago guy.

Bettors were both up and out of their seats on every play, screaming for the Celtics to score and then defend. With ten seconds to play, a questionable traveling call turned the ball over to the Celtics. Next, the official called a foul on a desperation three-point shot attempt by a clumsy Celtic bench player who last saw game action during the Reagan presidency. His off-balance heave had no chance to go in. Normally, fans would leave the game at this point because the outcome was certain, a win for the Bucks, a loss to the Celtics. Not so among these bettors, who were more interested in the spread than the average fan.

The Celtic player missed the first free throw, bricked the second, and lined up to shoot what appeared to be a meaningless free throw. Barbara was on her feet, bellowing at the television set. She was sweating like a racetrack horse and throwing down drinks side by side with Mr. Chicago.

The final free throw bounced around the rim and went in, after which the Bucks raced down the court and a long pass was deflected out of bounds as the game ended.

The Celtics covered the spread. Barbara had won again, and I was vindicated. The big bettor from Chicago could hardly speak. He slumped in his chair, the color drained from his perpetual tan. When he staggered to his feet, he slapped hands with Barbara, grunted a goodbye, and walked off a little crooked, like he was recovering from a stroke.

Barbara was lathered up, drained, and excited at the same time. She called a girlfriend and told her how much she had won in Vegas. That wasn't enough so she called her agent. She called room service, then changed her mind and called again. She called an old actor boyfriend while she took a bath. When she calmed down a bit, we had one of our one-way conversations.

Barbara: (leering) "I wish you were a guy right now. I'd make sure we had a night you would never forget. Of course, I could go down to the casino and take my pick of studs, but I could also wind up with an HIV carrier or some guy who would sell a story to the tabloids, or just make a pest of himself later. I promised myself I was through with bad choices."

She proceeded to put on a nightgown, turn on the monster TV with a thousand channels, and brought out the velvet box. She did not close the bedroom door, so I took it as an invitation to come in as a reward for my efforts. This time, she talked to me as she rubbed the penis-shaped object between her legs. For once she was not in a hurry, and I noticed that the buzzing sound it made was not unlike the buzzing of a fly.

I approached cautiously, landing gently on her slender, milky shoulder. The aromas rising from her body, part sweat, perfume, fruit, body lotion, and the mysterious sex scent, about did me in. This was it for me. I could have died right there and gone to fly heaven without a single regret.

Barbara: "Fly, you know what's happening, don't you? I don't even care how weird this is. Maybe you're a Martian. I don't care. This is more fun than any boyfriend I ever had. Or girlfriend for that matter. I know you love me, and you don't ask for anything, maybe some fruit and a little safety. That's not much to ask, is it? And nobody knows what you can do, or how smart you are, just me."

"You're my dirty little secret, my secret weapon. So, what if I let you touch me? You even sound like the vibrator. Ah, this is sweet. You're sweet you lovely, beautiful fly. If I could just make a man out of you. God knows I tried with some guys and they weren't half as smart as you."

I got up close to her ear and buzzed in a way I had never buzzed before. It was more musical, higher pitched, almost like a song. I was telling her that I wanted to be a man and do the things I had seen her boyfriend do with her, only it would be different because I loved her beyond words, of which I had none. I told her of my pain and longing, that we were species that could never be joined.

Barbara: (murmuring) "Fly, sing to me, sing to me."

I went into a vocal range I didn't know was possible. More humming than buzzing, high notes, low notes, sad and lonely notes. The television was on, but shutting down for the night, and the station was playing a song over a flag shown blowing in the wind.

I realized that I was humming the "Star-Spangled Banner", and just as it ended, Barbara shuddered, moaned, and dropped into a deep sleep.

Chapter 11
Love Walks In

I helped Barbara make some money, but aside from that, she really didn't need much help from me. Her career took off like a bottle rocket just about the time I crawled out of that dumpster at Gelson's. Money itself had ceased to be an issue as her fees were escalating faster than an insect reproduces.

It was the thrill of outsmarting the odds that appealed to her. Barbara was much smarter than her public, her agent, or anyone else realized. Much of the time, her intelligence terrorized the men she dated and she found it hard to sustain relationships with or take her actor and actress friends seriously. She played a lot of competitive bridge at a club in Santa Monica, and when I tried to tip her off to her opponent's cards, she just waved me off. She didn't want my help. She didn't need it.

When she wasn't working, she spent her spare time reading historical novels, biographies, magazines like The New Yorker, Wired, and of course, the endless scripts that poured in from her agent. When she decided to accept a role, she memorized her part by the second run-through. She managed to keep it all under wraps, playing the part of the not-terribly-smart, intellectually incurious, yet ambitious actress.

At home, she talked more and more to me, using me as a silent debate partner. Of course, I could never answer her, merely nod. I think she credited me with far more intelligence than I possessed, as I never had to argue any point with her or disagree with her on any subject. I did not formulate this as a strategy to enhance my credibility with her. It just happened due to my vocal limitation. The men in her life never seemed to grasp the benefit of this behavior, much to their detriment.

We half debated the wisdom of what roles to accept, both on television and in films. Eligible men and their various merits and weaknesses were discussed ad nauseam, as were agents, managers, lawyers, actors, directors, editors, and photographers. All of her talk was not restricted to "the business". She went on at some length about politics, art, music, business, literature, and culture. She provided me with an education of sorts while making no demands upon me to make any special use of that education.

As simplistic pundits might say, life was good. And then it changed in an instant. Barbara was making so much money her advisors were telling her to buy "bulletproof" real estate, meaning a larger house in Bel Air, Brentwood, or Pacific Palisades. Malibu was good too, but there was not a sufficient inventory of homes to choose from at the price level she was ready for.

Having decided to at least look into a new home, Barbara called a nationally known real estate company specializing in the high-end homes she was told to pursue. An appointment was made for one of their agents to come out to Malibu. It was his presence that changed everything.

He was tall, well-dressed in a casual way (tailored jeans and a very expensive Italian sports coat), polite, and not at all intimidated by Barbara's celebrity. He was in his mid-thirties and had dark, thick hair, a smooth complexion, bright blue eyes, square shoulders, and a narrow waist. He was very masculine, confident, apparently well-educated, and relaxed.

Barbara reacted as though her vital systems had been re-programmed. Her breathing was shallow, nearly panting. Her skin tone had reddened, her eyes were glazed, and her coordination seemed lacking. She offered him food and wine, and tripped over herself, eager to please, but confused at the same time.

He seemed to take it all in stride as if women always behaved this way in his presence. Maybe they did, for all I knew. It was kind of fascinating to see Barbara, always so cool and in control, become another person. She proceeded to spill things, search for things that were in plain sight, stumble over her words, trip over her own feet, and babble somewhat incoherently at times.

His name was Jeff, and he came prepared with a list of properties, videos with virtual tours, comparable sales data, neighborhood restrictions, traffic studies, air quality data, and the like. Barbara hung on every word. Jeff was in no hurry and seemed to enjoy the attention. He flattered Barbara with compliments as he went through his sales pitch. It was almost like a ritual dance that insects perform before mating, and I could see it developing moment by moment.

Jeff praised her taste in furniture, admired her choice of music, and loved the elegance of her house. He commented on the ocean breeze that stirred the delicate lace curtains made for her in Mexico. He noticed details like the Jade Buddha on her mantle; he had one just like it that he brought back from Nepal on his last mountain climbing adventure. Of course, Barbara wanted to know all the personal details she could mine from Jeff about his background.

Barbara: "You seem to know everything about Beverly Hills. Did you grow up there?"

Jeff: "No. I am originally from upstate New York"

Barbara: "Well, how did you get here?"

Jeff: "I went to UCLA for my Master's."

Barbara: "You must have majored in business. I understand the Anderson School has a wonderful reputation"

Jeff: (laughing) "No, I was a physics major at Cornell and I wanted to do my graduate work where it was sunny and warm."

Barbara: (murmuring) "Really, physics? I'm impressed."

Jeff: "So was I until I realized I could never make a decent living at it."

The verbal dance went on for hours until they were sitting side by side on the pastel green suede sofa, their legs brushing, her hands fluttering with the conversation, touching his arm, brushing back her hair nervously. I half expected them both to go up in flames, it was that hot.

Jeff had the good sense to slow things down by setting up his videos and talking shop, moving away from the sofa, and finally suggesting an early dinner at Wolfgang Puck's restaurant. Barbara went to her bedroom to change clothes, and I went with her. She whispered to me while she picked through her closet looking for the perfect outfit.

Barbara: "Fly, can you believe it, he's gorgeous and smart. I almost raped him. I think I still might do it."

She was looking at dresses, throwing them on the bed. She changed her underwear three times, determined to show her spectacular assets in the best possible light.

Barbara: (fussing) "Do you think he likes me?"

Ultimately, she pulled on a pair of skin-tight jeans, a tailored shirt, and a sports jacket. I wanted to tell her she was dressed exactly like Jeff.

Jeff: (in a reedy voice) "Are you talking to someone in there?"

Barbara: "No, no, it's just the radio."

She gave me a conspiratorial nod, burst into the living room, and locked me in the bedroom without a backward glance. It was a portent of things to come.

In the weeks that followed, Jeff and Barbara became inseparable. The inevitable happened with Jeff bedding Barbara (or maybe it was the other way around) by their third date. After that, Barbara's schedule changed, and she began a different round of activities. She met Jeff's friends, went to Laker games with Jeff, and attended rock concerts and jazz clubs.

All the conversation about politics, culture, social change, and international affairs that she used to share with me was now directed to Jeff. Since he could respond, the conversations were far more satisfying to Barbara. I was the odd man out, so to speak, relegated to my former position of merely being a fly on the wall.

Jeff was at our house when he wasn't working and he was there most nights. Barbara was shooting more and more shows, either television or films. She had photo shoots for magazine covers, and interviews with talk shows, radio, and TV. They were on the road to becoming a "power couple".

Jeff was showing her houses in LA's best west side neighborhoods. Huge spreads with acres of lawn and trees, Olympic-size swimming pools, video game rooms, billiard rooms, screening rooms, bowling alleys, security gates, wine cellars, themed guest suites, workout rooms, indoor basketball and squash courts, industrial-sized kitchens, sophisticated security and communication systems, and ballrooms for entertaining upwards of 100 guests. Barbara would take me along when she met Jeff and I would fly through these monuments to excess, unguarded and unseen. My wings ached from flying so much and that was only indoors.

Barbara wanted to please Jeff, but she was uncertain about acquiring one of these Beverly Hills behemoths. Nobody mentioned that it would require a staff of at least 10 people to manage the maintenance of these monstrosities. She only relaxed when she returned to her modest Malibu house and when we were alone, she would ask me whether I liked one house or the other. Unable to respond, the questions were mostly rhetorical and only served to underline her uncertainty.

Jeff did not press her, but neither did he stop the showings. At one point they called a moratorium on showings for an indeterminate time.

One afternoon Barbara met Jeff at his office in Beverly Hills, and I went along. She parked herself in the waiting room while I quietly explored the inner chambers. There were several offices in a U shape, all with windows that looked out on the streets below. Most had large, ornate desks, wall charts filled with names and sales information, the standard computer, printer, copier machines, and flat-screen televisions. The walls either had original art or tasteful prints hung between polished wooden bookcases.

In the middle of a U-shaped glass-framed conference room, Jeff was engaged in a heated conversation with a short middle-aged man wearing a dark pin-striped suit and a flag pin in his lapel. He might as well have had a sign on his prominent forehead, stating that he was the boss.

Boss: "Jeff, when are you going to close a deal with this girl?"

Jeff: "I can't rush her. I'm doing everything I can."

Boss: "You're not showing her enough of our listings. I don't give a shit about Coldwell's listings or Prudential's, they're all bullshit to me."

Jeff: "I have to cover the whole market. She needs to see everything in her price range."

Boss: "Bullshit, this is taking way too long. Are you afraid that once she buys a house, you can't schtup her anymore? "

Jeff: "This is not about my personal life, don't go there."

Boss: "Everyone knows you're banging this girl; why do you think we sent you there? You never complained about being the office whore before."

Jeff: "Is that what you think I am?"

Boss: "Fuck yes, and you're good at it. Don't forget I saw your potential when you were selling used cars to horny Valley housewives for peanuts. I brought you here and trained you. I gave you that Ivy League education story that our buyers love so much. I don't know what you told this latest one, but it sure wasn't the truth."

Jeff: "You wouldn't blow my story, would you?"

Boss: "Nah, you make this sale, I get big dollars. And, she looks like a piece of ass made by God himself, so live it up, kid. But close the deal."

I had heard enough of this conversation, although I didn't know what I would or should do with it. Jeff was not the person Barbara thought he was. I still wasn't sure exactly who he was, but that didn't make a difference because he was lying to her right from the start.

I needed to get out of the glassed-in conference room without delay, but that wasn't so easy. I would have avoided that room had I not seen Jeff and his manager going toe to toe. It was worth the risk because they were so involved, they were not likely to notice me. But once they broke up, I felt exposed.

I stayed low on the floor, flew from chair to chair, and when the manager left the room, I was right behind him at shoe-top level. I flew right into Barbara's purse; the top was always left open for me. I didn't want to see Jeff and I didn't want him to see me. They went to dinner and then Jeff drove his own car out to Malibu afterward.

I kept to myself while Jeff and Barbara had their after-dinner drinks, watched the end of a Laker game, groped one another affectionately, and then headed for the bedroom. It was life as usual, except I knew something that was likely to disrupt this cozy picture.

I still did not know how I could tell Barbara the bad news, or even if I should tell her the bad news. There were times - and this was one - when it was nerve-wracking to know the real character of someone who could hurt the person you cherished.

Chapter 12
Fear

How do you go about wrecking someone's relationship, carrying unhappiness like a plague, bearing secrets that humiliate one person and hurt another? I didn't hold any ill will toward Jeff, even though he had taken a big chunk of Barbara away from me. I was objective enough to know that Barbara needed men in her life, and that I was a curiosity destined to provide some amusement and occasionally some useful information, but not much more. My situation reminded me of a movie I had seen on late-night television.

Jeff and Barbara had left the TV on as they made their way to the bedroom in a state of mutual inflammation. Cyrano de Bergerac, gargantuan nose preceding his every move, spoke to my sense of isolation. His deformity had made him a unique creature, gifted though he was. His love for Roxanne would never be returned, that was certain. His honesty, his purity, and his devotion only earned him the right to suffer.

The stuff of tragedy, but for a fly, not even that. Does anyone take a fly seriously? I doubt it. I too would suffer in silence like Cyrano, locked in my fly's body, unable to speak my feelings. Me and Cyrano: repulsive, rejected, and replaced by lesser men. This was something new for me, drosophila depression disorder. Perhaps the answer would be to linger in someone's therapy sessions and see if I could get something out of it for myself.

I could expose Jeff as a liar and a fraud and that would send Barbara right to a shrink. It was cruel to even think that way. I decided she would have to find out for herself, although I could try and protect her. Meanwhile, I would deal with my own depression by sneaking into some therapy sessions that were available to me.

Barbara was seeing a dentist in a large medical building in Westwood. I started going with her as we had evolved a communication style for travel. If she wanted me to go, I would fly into the top of her purse where she had arranged a comfortable little pocket for me. If not, I would stay at home while she went about her business and she would leave food for me.

The medical building where Barbara went for her appointments had the usual number of dentists, medical specialists, and shrinks of all stripes. No insect specialists, although the infectious disease guys might qualify. Not being able to read the plaques on the doors, I had to rely on a trial-and-error method. I was able to eliminate many of the offices by simply observing the people who entered them. Patients in wheelchairs, and those with canes and crutches, told me what I needed to know. The offices with in-patient surgical facilities were also eliminated.

Finally, I learned that the shrinks had waiting rooms with comfortable furniture, generally no receptionist, only a button pressed by the patient to announce his or her presence to the shrink in his or her inner office.

I lingered in many waiting rooms before finding the right situation. I had the time because Barbara was undergoing a lengthy treatment for her teeth, which had been neglected by her parents during her childhood. She had grown up on a ranch in rural Texas and dentists were not nearby, nor were her parents much concerned. They had four other siblings to deal with after Barbara's birth and it was all they could do to keep up with the serious injuries. Good teeth were a luxury in Texas, but a necessity in Hollywood.

The patient I selected to monitor was a woman in her late forties, attractive, well-dressed in a conservative way, and very nervous. The moment she entered the interior office she started talking and kept at it for her fifty minutes. The shrink barely got in a word, mostly nodded and made notes.

She had fears about everything from death and HIV infection to mold in her bathroom. She had been married for twenty years, but wasn't sure if her husband was infecting her with some sexually transmitted disease, even though she was certain he was not cheating on her.

Food was another source of her fears: chickens could give you salmonella, spinach was contaminated by E. coli bacteria, and she spotted red marks on nearly every can, package, or container and thought it might be blood. Everyone who waited on her at the supermarket had an open sore on his or her hand or face that could be a source of transmission if he touched her or touched her packages.

She washed her hands fifty times a day and argued with her husband and children endlessly over the need to wash or disinfect. Dirt was her sworn enemy, so she fired her cleaning women every two weeks because they did not clean or sanitize every inch of her excessively large home to her satisfaction.

There were times when she forgot to remove her thin rubber gloves when going to bed and had to be reminded to take them off. She was reluctant to do so.

This woman wasn't crazy, but fear was driving her life. Her family was unable to function due to her inability to deal with food. Going out for meals was not much better as she cross-examined the waiters and waitresses about the particulars of the food on the menu. Was the sauce meat-based? Were the vegetables locally grown? Who handled the food that was put on the plate? Was the cheese free of rennet? Was the kitchen regularly inspected for bugs and cleanliness, to merit an A rating? Was the fish farm-raised, or wild-caught? Was the chicken free range? Was the meat from the cattle free of BES? Was the water filtered? Had she known there was a fly in the room with her she would have triple-sprayed every inch of the room with the Lysol can she kept in her purse.

I could have told her some things about fear. A fly has mortal enemies everywhere. Most of us don't have any kind of shelter, let alone ten thousand square foot houses. The real fear is knowing that every human being sees nothing wrong with murdering a fly that wanders into his or her orbit.

The insect world is none too friendly either. There are as many varieties of spiders as there are flies, all of them looking at you as tonight's meal. Dogs, cats, rats, it's all the same, whether they crush you, eat you, beat you with a tail or a tongue. It's like welcoming a known assassin into your home. You can never relax at any moment until the killer is dispatched, is shown the door, or decides to pursue other victims.

Capture by a well-meaning researcher is even worse. Tear off his wings, induce a deadly disease, interfere with his fertility, it's all okay, he's just another fly.

I wonder what this shrink would think if he heard my tale?

Fear was the order of the day. After the patient departed, the shrink got on his phone and started in with a colleague about terrorists and more fear. I leaned in a little closer to the phone to overhear the full conversation.

Shrink one: "We've never had an enemy like this in all of our history."

Shrink two: "They're unique, but they're disorganized, low tech, and divided amongst themselves."

Shrink one: "Pakistan has the bomb, and their people hate us enough to pull the trigger. Same with Iran, if they have the bomb. If either country did it, they would be the heroes of the entire Arab world. The next best thing would be to drop the bomb on the Israelis. Later, they could claim it was a mistake to avoid retaliation."

Shrink two: "Do you believe they want to provoke a world war - because that would be the consequence? We'd have to retaliate."

Shrink one: "Who said it first - maybe it was Barry Goldwater - we should bomb them into the Stone Age."

Shrink two: "They're already in the stone age so it wouldn't make much difference. That's what they want; to go back to the conditions of the 7th century."

Shrink one: "Now that would put us out of business."

Shrink two: "That's the best argument I've heard to drop the bomb."

Shrink one: "We should put Prozac in their water system."

Shrink two: "They don't have any water systems. We should infiltrate their culture with hookers. It's all about sex and repression."

Shrink one: "I doubt the hookers would work the refugee camps."

Shrink two: "One bad sexual performance could lead to a beheading. Too risky."

Shrink one: "I guess that leaves us with diplomacy."

Shrink two: "That works for the Stone Age mind."

Shrink one: "How about sending them our prison population?"

Shrink two: "We call them Blackwater and they're already in Iraq. Of course, they failed there. We'd do better to pull out the Army and let the mercenaries have at it."

Shrink one: "I think we should stick to solving our patients' problems."

Shrink two: "Unfortunately, we're not doing much better there than we are in the Middle East."

This was truly discouraging. I didn't get much that would help me from the therapy sessions, and I got even less from the political discussion.

My only conclusion was that fear is everywhere so get used to it. I would have to live without herapy.

Chapter 13
Love Walks Out

Barbara completed her cosmetic dentistry about the same time I gave up on therapy. Shortly afterward, she and Jeff attended a Lakers game, now a part of their social ritual. Although I was not invited, I snuck into Barbara's purse, curious to attend this spectacle I had only glimpsed on television.

Jeff had seats close to the floor and a parking pass that enabled him to park his red sports car practically inside the arena itself. The game had already begun when we were ushered through a noisy, densely packed crowd of flamboyantly dressed men and women in furs and leathers. No animal rights people at this gathering.

Some people were watching the game unfold below them in the brightly lit arena, but most seemed to be watching one another, even themselves on the jumbo television screen hung from the rafters above mid-court. Jeff waved to a couple being shown to their seats, the man stumbling because his eyes were glued to Barbara in her seat. The couple was seated next to a famous older actress accompanied by a much younger rock musician, whose hair was considerably longer than his date.

Being so close to the court, many of the spectators, celebrities, and players seemed to either know or recognize one another. When a referee made a questionable call and assessed a penalty, there was a barrage of eye rolls exchanged with the players. A good play, a ferocious dunk for instance, always got a thumbs up from the audience, a roar of approval, followed by a nod or a hand sign recognized by the player.

During time outs, and there were plenty of those to accommodate the television sponsors, there would be an occasional fist bump from a player or a hand slap with a celebrity fan while the team gathered around their coach and assistants. Up close the players, who looked more or less normal on a television screen, were far from ordinary.

Even those players of normal height and size appeared to be members of a tribe from an entirely different species. Their hands and feet were enormous, their bodies sculpted, their movements graceful and self-assured. Sweat poured from them in rivers and buckets, mopped up by trainers and assistants. A tribal language, heavy on profanity, nicknames, abbreviations, and linguistic shortcuts served as communication between the men, both on and off the court, as the game progressed.

I was unprepared for the noise that accompanied the game in its live format. The players talked to one another and their opponents non-stop. They pushed, shoved, grunted, and collided with one another. The impact of all this activity was felt as much as heard. When a special or important play happened, the crowd's approval burst like a wave of sound upon the court.

At each break in the game, there were dance teams of barely-clad girls flooding the court, and music blasting from speakers. There were announcements, giveaway prizes, and contests where fans came onto the court to win some money or a modest trip by throwing the ball from half-court into the basket. It was a high-energy, high-pitched, large, randomly selected multi-racial Los Angeles party.

While the ongoing racket was disconcerting, it offered me a kind of freedom. All the overlapping activity, to say nothing of the drinking, eating, cheering, pointing, fist-bumping, high-fiving, and ogling of movie stars made my presence virtually invisible. At halftime, I snuck away from the purse and made a tour of the arena, lost in the constantly moving crowd, a restless mass of bodies searching out bathrooms, friends, food vendors, and players, most on their cell phones at the same time.

Behind the Lakers' bench, I recognized a face, framed by a tweed, short-billed cap, that I had seen up close. It belonged to the giant who owned the pickup truck that had been carelessly smashed by a red sports car driven by the young man so captivated by his own hair. Come to think of it, the man who fled from the scene of the accident he caused, looked a whole lot like Jeff,

Barbara's current boyfriend. Until now I had never connected Jeff to that accident.

When the man took off his cap, he was nearly bald, his hair only a monk's fringe on the sides and back. This verified to me that he was the owner of the truck whose front had been demolished and the person who stared me down as a potential witness.

He was every bit the size of the largest players on the court, but appeared to be at least twice their age. He held a pad and clipboard on which he was writing notes. He walked with a slight limp to speak to the Lakers coach and his assistant coaches, while glancing at his notes. He belonged here as more than a fan; he was in some way related to the Lakers team.

I approached cautiously to confirm my conclusion, staying low and out of sight for the most part. My quarry no longer stood out as a giant in the context of the basketball team. They were all huge, and it occurred to me that they were mutants, just like me, but at the other end of the weight and size spectrum.

Sure enough, the man spotted me perched on the side of an empty courtside chair. He said nothing but looked directly at me. At first, it was a short glance, but then he turned back to look again and stared at me until he smiled and nodded at me. He gestured at a nearby exit, the tunnel where the players had left the court for their dressing rooms at halftime. The corridor was empty, the only quiet place in the building.

He kept his voice low and didn't look directly at me, so it would not appear that a conversation was taking place.

Giant: (growling while looking down at his clipboard) "What you doing here, you little motherfucker? I know you ain't no basketball fan. You must be doin' okay, a little bigger and fatter and goin' to Laker games like some hotshot."

Of course, I could not answer, but I buzzed as loud as I could and flew out and back several times to see if he got the idea that I wanted him to follow me. He was unsure at first but got my drift, and we left the building through a private exit and into the parking lot.

I led him to Jeff's red sports car, which he recognized instantly. A beatific smile lit up his face, followed by a burst of profanity, which I had come to expect as a member of his tribe. He circled the sports car several times to be sure it was the right car, and sure enough, when he brushed off the dirt there was the license plate exactly as I recalled it, $RES. He scratched off a little gray paint hiding near the license plate that had not been fully covered. He then delivered a vicious booted kick to the driver's side of the car.

Giant: "This is the dude that hit me, no doubt about it. I'd like to get my baseball bat and beat this car into a Campbell's soup can, but that would be too easy. I got to meet this dude before I file a police report on this motherfucker, hit-and-run motherfucker is what he is. I got to go back to work, but you meet me here after the game."

After a moment, he added, turning in my direction, "Some fun this gonna be."

He walked back into the arena, smiling. Over his shoulder, he looked back at me.

Giant: "I owe you one, you little mother-fucker, I do."

I found my way back to Barbara, and into her purse without incident. She was clinging to Jeff, who was only marginally interested in the ball game. Instead, he was pitching a real estate deal to the couple seated behind him. When the game ended with a Laker win, the two couples lingered while the men exchanged business cards, made a little small talk, and departed separately. I cowered in my hideaway, uncertain of what I had set in motion.

Jeff and Barbara strolled arm in arm to their VIP parking space, where the giant was seated on the hood of the sports car, tapping the front fender with a baseball bat he removed from his locker in the dressing room. Every enforcer needs one. He was accompanied by a younger man of almost the same size who I recognized as a Laker player who sat on the bench and did not play in the game. The giant rose to his feet and towered over Jeff and Barbara. He abandoned his usual slouch and seemed to rise like a building to peer down at Jeff as if he were an insect on the sidewalk. I know the feeling.

Giant: "Nice car you got here dude. You own this ride?"

He said this in a friendly conversational tone of voice. He didn't wait for a reply.

Giant: "I been looking for a car just like this."

Jeff: (confidently) "Hey, what is this, a carjacking? You guys want to steal my car, is that right?

Giant: "No man, how could we fit in this little thing? You think the two of us carjack you by picking it up and carrying it away?"

Both the giant and the Laker player broke up laughing and high-fived one another. Barbara said nothing, but I knew that wouldn't last for long.

Barbara looked up at the Giant and the Laker. "You're scaring us, aren't you? This is childish and if it keeps up, I'll call the police and we'll find out what this is all about."

Giant: (still tapping his baseball bat against the car) "Well darlin' why don't you just do that? Get out your iPhone and dial up the local police and we'll explain that I just located the honky that busted up the front of my truck, damned near killed me before he left the scene of the accident, and forgot to leave me his name, address, and telephone number, so I could find his chickenshit ass and bust him."

Barbara: "Jeff, what is he talking about? Do you know this man?"

Jeff failed to answer. His head was swiveling around in a desperate search for help, but the parking lot was clearing rapidly and the other drivers had windows up and rushed to the exits. The only help would have to come from security stationed within the arena. The giant raised his fingers to his mouth and let out an ear-splitting whistle as he beckoned to one of the security personnel at the VIP entrance.

Jeff: (shouting) "No, no. Do you want money, is that it? I've got $200 on me, you can have it, just leave us alone."

The two black men roared with laughter.

Giant: "Two hundred bucks; you think we're street punks?"

Younger player: (laughing) "Two hundred bucks!"

They laughed as they high-fived again.

Barbara nearly crushed me as she jammed her hand into the purse, looking for her iPhone. When the giant got his laughter under control, he turned to Barbara and then explained.

Giant: "I was parked outside the CBS lot on a side street and this car driven by your husband smashed into me in his red sports car, knocked me unconscious, seriously damaged my pickup truck, and was nowhere to be found when I came to. He left no information, which the law requires.

Go ahead and make the call. Be sure to add this was a hit-and-run accident, with personal injuries and property damage. There is a paint transfer on the rear bumper of his car that matches the paint on the front of my truck. His rear bumper has been cheaply repaired to cover over the damage but the paint transfer is still there."

Barbara: "Just a minute. If he smashed into you, the damage to your car would be to the rear and his car would be damaged in the front, not the rear."

Barbara was not one to back down without a satisfactory explanation, while Jeff remained mute and shuffled his feet, still hoping to find an escape route.

Giant: "This accident happened because your husband..."

Barbara: (interrupting) "Not my husband."

Giant: "Okay, your boyfriend was parallel parked in front of me and was too busy combing his hair and talking on his cell phone to realize that his transmission was in reverse, and he smashed down his accelerator and crashed directly into the front of my truck. That is how the accident happened. I can identify him because I saw him directly before the collision, and I recognize the car he was driving.

Giant: (pointing his bat towards Jeff's car) "And this is it."

Jeff: (in a voice several octaves higher than his normal baritone) "I can explain, I can. I'm just shook up. These guys are shaking me down. I don't know them. I don't know anything about some truck. I just bought this car, and it must have been someone else you're looking for, and the guy never told me about any accident. This has nothing to do with me, it's all a mistake."

Jeff: (pointing at the Giant) "I didn't do anything wrong, this guy made up some crazy story. It wasn't me, it wasn't my car, I wasn't there, I never saw this guy before."

Giant: (pulling on his tweed cap) "You want to play the game this way, is that it? You have a red signet ring on your right hand and I'm guessing it's still there. Stick out your hand and let me see it."

Jeff's response was to shove his right hand deep into his pants pocket.

Barbara: (in a calm voice) "Let's see your hand, Jeff."

He reluctantly extended his right hand to Barbara, the ring right where he always wore it.

Jeff: (whimpering) "It was a lucky guess, that's all it was."

Giant: "No, it wasn't a guess. I saw that ring reflect the light when you had your arm up combing your hair for fifteen minutes, and I know the vanity plate on your car. It's $RES. What does that stand for? Say, Jack, what business are you in? Got a business card on you right now?"

Jeff: (more evenly) "No, I'm all out of cards. I'm in the financial business," said Jeff evenly.

She turned to the two men.

Barbara: (pointing at the Giant) "He's in the real estate business, if that matters. Give him your card, Jeff, and he can figure out what it means."

Laker player: (to no one in particular) "We got a beautiful, honest, unmarried woman here."

That comment sent Jeff off. He started hollering and threatening the two men with false imprisonment, kidnapping, sexual harassment, assault and battery, trespass, and every legal term he could think of.

The recipients of the threats were unmoved, and worse for Jeff, Barbara had apparently switched sides. She insisted that everyone exchange names, addresses, phone numbers, insurance information, and the photo she took of the vanity plate on her phone.

She told the older man that she would have her lawyer contact him tomorrow to discuss whether the matter could be resolved without police involvement. She understood that Jeff was understandably surprised, but he would make good on any damage he caused unintentionally. She guaranteed it. She entered the Giant's information on her iPhone.

Jeff was silent and remained so on the ride back to Malibu. He did not stay the night. As Barbara got out of the car, she turned and confronted Jeff.

Barbara: "Don't ever lie to me about anything."

We didn't hear much from Jeff after the damage case was settled.

Chapter 14
New York

Not long after Jeff had been put on hold, pending final dismissal for perjury, Barbara landed her first starring role in a big-time Hollywood feature film, to be shot on location in New York and Washington D.C. I thought, at first, I might be left behind, but Barbara thought otherwise.

She flew to New York in a private studio jet and stayed in the Trump Towers. To secure my presence and protect both of us from detection, my place in her purse had been specially designed with a mesh pocket on top that allowed air in, but hid my presence. The bottom of the space was padded for comfort and even had a food compartment into which Barbara was kind enough to insert tasty morsels for my enjoyment and nutrition. The purse had been acoustically insulated by a prominent acoustical engineer so that my buzzing sounds were absorbed by the material.

It had not been easy to explain her requirements to the leather craftsman who fashioned the purse. This same bag was also battery-heated, as Barbara knew that an East Coast winter would be a challenge for me. You just don't see fruit flies cruising around in a blizzard or fighting over garbage in sub-freezing temperatures.

Barbara carried her purse wherever she went, so I had the full tour of New York when she wasn't busy with costume fittings, rehearsals, cocktail parties, director's meetings, publicity shots, and the like. She was busy and energized and had little time for me, so I was left to my own devices.

I was cautious and more than a little disoriented at first. Barbara's Malibu place was the only home I had ever known and although her apartment in the Trump Towers was luxurious and spacious, it was a change. People were always coming in unexpectedly whether it was room service, maids, mail service, housekeeping with fresh clothing, or trash collection. There was diminished privacy, and I had to be constantly on alert for some new face who might be hostile to flies.

Flies were a rarity in this cold weather and I began to miss the presence of flies even though I had little to do with them in LA. It was the idea of flies; seeing them, knowing they were out there, that gave me a sense of normalcy.

Here, I was a sideshow freak, a one-of-a-kind, conspicuous like a dark stain on a white background. With Barbara gone so much and strangers everywhere I was homesick, lost, disconnected, and desperate. I had no choice; I had to take some risks to preserve my sanity.

One morning I climbed into Barbara's purse to escape the apartment, fully meaning to fend for myself in New York. Barbara was doing a reading with the other principal cast members at a theater in mid-town Manhattan.

It wasn't a terrible day for winter, just cold, certainly not a California day.

When everyone was engaged in the reading I slipped out of the purse, flew out the door, and headed for the restaurant next door. It was a steamy deli, filled with people in overcoats and scarves, intent on their food and seemingly heedless of my presence. I managed to relax, even steal a few bites of a pastrami sandwich left on a plate by the rear door. There were garbage cans outside, and to my surprise, a few bedraggled flies perched on the lip of the cans.

I approached buzzing nonchalantly, as though I did this every day. It was the lure of companionship, not food, that drew me into the orbit of these insects that I normally ignored. I had nearly forgotten the language of flies, the intonations of the buzz, the variations in pitch and volume that were a substitute for words. I listened carefully; these New York flies had their own dialect. Their buzzing was blunt, somewhat nasal, and came in staccato-like bursts. Not surprisingly, food and sex were the constant topics.

I overcame my disgust at the messy garbage cans and lingered on the lip, next to a young female fly with nice wings. Wings, in the world of the fly, have the same mysterious attraction that breasts have in the human world. A really sweet pair of wings, nicely shaped, not scarred or droopy, thin, diaphanous, and close to the body, is extremely provocative. Maybe the rest of the body is not so great; lumpy, too hairy, missing a leg or two, but the right wings can make all that go away. My eyes were riveted on her wings and I felt the stirring in my gut that had long been absent.

Up from the innards of the stinking refuse container came the alpha male fly, almost as big as myself. He was a real veteran of the streets, full of assertiveness and attitude. Immediately, he grasped the situation; my interest in the desirable young female, the outstanding wings that would someday inspire thousands of sex-crazed flies, and the hesitation of the teen-age girl fly.

"You're mine," the big fly buzzed confidently. "Give it up here and now."

"Not here in front of everyone," she begged off shyly.

"No difference to me," he insisted.

"Give her a break," I interjected.

The big fly answered "Who the fuck are you? I've never seen you around here. Fuck off before I bust your furry ass."

This was all new to me, the threat of violence, the hidden prize of sex behind it. I wasn't sure I wanted any part of this confrontation, but some instinct made me stay to play my part. I puffed up my chest, spread out my wings, and beat them menacingly. I stared and flared my eyes, rising to my full, well-fed size. My rival must have realized that I was the biggest, most imposing fly he had ever encountered.

"She's mine, tough guy," I spit out.

The big fly grunted, "I'll have her tomorrow."

I retorted, "Get out of here or you won't see tomorrow."

I had no clue where this dialogue came from, probably late-night television, but it certainly affected the object of our conflict. The young and juicy female fluttered those lovely wings at me and I knew exactly what it meant.

"Let's get out of here," I said to her.

She blinked and followed me into the restaurant, close behind, watching my every move. We stopped briefly for a last bite of the pastrami, then headed for the door. We flew together down the long hallway, stopping only to rub up against one another, and then to the room where Barbara's reading was still in progress. Her purse was open, and we flew into my hiding space without anyone the wiser.

It was warm and dark and whetted our mutual appetite for sex. But she was nervous, not knowing where she was or who she was with.

Right off, she wanted to get out and go back to her garbage can. I had to calm her fears, soothe her precious wings, and assert my masculine control without seeming too aggressive. I told her in so many words that she was about to go to fly heaven, a warm and loving environment where the humans in charge meant us no harm and instead provided us with shelter and food.

I was dead wrong on all counts. When Barbara returned to her apartment, it did not take long for her to discover that I had female company. I came out of the purse with little Miss Wings emerging a beat later. Barbara recoiled at the sight of another insect.

Barbara: (evenly) "Fly, what is this? What have you brought into my apartment?"

Being unable to answer I moved closer to Wings, shielding her from Barbara's rising anger.

Barbara: "You have no right to bring your uninvited guests to my place. This is not a home for wayward insects."

Wings was shaking and looking for an escape route, as any sensible fly would do under the circumstances.

Barbara's voice was rising, an emotional outburst on the way. I wondered if jealousy could be in play.

Barbara: "Just because I befriended you, it's not okay to bring home any insect of your choice.

Maybe you would like to bring home a tarantula, or a scorpion just for company. I see what you want, it's sex with this miserable little creature. You fertilize her eggs for your pleasure and the next thing I know, there are five or six hundred flies in my place. Is that what you want?"

I hadn't thought about it that way. Now I was torn between the need to protect Wings, the newly minted desire for sex, and my dependence on Barbara. I treasured the luxury and safety of my life with Barbara; I didn't want to give it up. Barbara could and would put me out on the street without hesitation should I cross her. I was temporarily saved by the phone.

Barbara: "Don't move until I'm off the phone. And no quickies here; you stay away from that little slut." She spoke to me like an angry parent to a wayward teenager.

The phone call was from Jeff in Los Angeles. Barbara hesitated before taking the call, but relented to speak with the liar. Mostly, she listened as Jeff pitched her to come home to see the perfect house, then switched to saying he would come to New York. Both plans were diplomatically vetoed.

Jeff's ship was sailing away, only he was slow to recognize it. My ship didn't look much better.

I flew toward the door with Wings trailing me, and Barbara let us out, with instructions for me to come back inside in an hour. She made it clear that I should come back alone. Wings followed me out, but I knew right off when we stopped for a break in the downstairs lobby that something was wrong.

"She talked to you and you understood her," she sniffed.

"Yeah, I guess so."

"Whadda' you mean, you guess so. You live with her!"

"Okay, so I live with her."

"You're a freak, and you scare me. I want to go home."

"Home's a garbage can in an alley behind a deli!"

"You don't have to go there. Go back to your woman!"

My sexual adventure had turned into a nasty argument. I was shocked at how quickly Wings had changed direction, but I was still determined to see this through. I decided to be more direct because flies are realists for the most part, having little time to waste on niceties.

"Let's fly back to the deli and have sex now," I blurted.

"No, no, no," was her answer. "You're not even a real fly. You're some kind of a weird pet. She probably feeds you steroids or something to make you so big. Go away and leave me alone."

And off she went, her lovely wings shimmering in the glow of the lobby fixtures. My bubble of superiority had been popped. I would have to be more careful in the selection of a sexual partner, somebody not so young, more experienced, more tolerant of differences, and more open to new situations and lifestyles. It probably wouldn't have worked out anyway.

We lived in different worlds. She would be burned out shortly, the mother of hundreds of offspring, her exquisite wings reduced to pulpy flaps, dead or dying within a matter of weeks, while I continued to flourish in good health in Malibu. Oh, but it would have been sweet.

Maybe Jeff felt the same way I did. Rudely dismissed, no hope of repairing the situation.

Chapter 15
The White House

After the Wings fiasco, Barbara seemed a little more considerate of my situation. She seemed to understand that I was bored and limited in what I could do while she was occupied with her work. She made some excuses so we could go shopping and I could roam around the stores, the shopping malls, the trendy boutiques, and the glitzy hotels. I was looking for an opportunity to be useful to Barbara again, and it wasn't coming easy.

Meanwhile, Eric, the film's director, had received a surprise invitation to dine at the White House. Probably all the publicity that the cast and crew had generated in New York was the explanation. Dinner would be at 7:30, preceded by a reception so invited guests could mingle. It all came to pass very quickly, with Barbara and Eric representing the film.

The short flight from JFK to Dulles deposited us in Washington D.C., in what seemed like minutes. We checked into our hotel, and Eric and Barbara took a break in preparation for the evening ahead. Barbara primped and puttered and dressed for the occasion. She was nothing short of stunning in a designer gown she purchased in New York from an up-and-coming, but still obscure designer.

After leaving the hotel in a taxi, we cleared security at the White House and were shown into a large room adjacent to the formal guest dining room.

Barbara sparkled in a setting that glittered in every way, from the furniture to the table settings to the people themselves. Even the waiters looked like movie stars or spoke as if they had PhDs. It seemed like I had seen photographs of most of the guests in some newspaper, magazine, or television show.

Barbara and Eric fit smoothly into the reception, but I was uncomfortable in a crowd. My real desire was to explore the White House. I flew down the polished hallways, covered in rich oriental carpets, past offices with the usual computer gear, alongside walls covered with historical photographs and paintings by famous artists.

At one point, I lingered in a windowless room where a young male nerd bent over a computer, straining to create a document in an undecipherable computer code. I didn't buzz or interfere with his duties, but merely observed his lonely struggles while the music from the reception room drifted down the hallways.

Not in my wildest dreams did I imagine this moment would result in a near catastrophe for me and Barbara.

I moved on innocently to the Oval Office. It looked exactly like the one on the old West Wing television show. Barbara watched the re-runs religiously. There in formal dress were the President and Vice President sitting on a leather sofa, deciding the fate of the world. True to my instincts, I took up a position on the wall behind the sofa eager to eavesdrop, expecting these two exalted figures to utter words of wisdom I would never forget. They were discussing the president's morning briefing. In the background a giant flat-screen television blared away, permanently set to Fox News at high volume:

POTUS: "Ya' know these briefings are too damn long. I told these boys to cut it down so I could read it before I finished breakfast. I want it even shorter than Bush or Reagan had it."

VP: "Neither of them read it anyway, didn't need to."

POTUS: "They make 'em so damned complicated. Worse than reading the New York Times. I gave that up years ago for Fox News."

VP: "Biggest waste of time on the planet. Fake news. You nailed it there, boss; you've got a gift for coining issues and labeling people."

POTUS: "Crooked Hillary, the whole country loves it. Lock her up."

VP: "I love it. Keep it up, boss. Good thing you kicked her ass in the election. Can you imagine that woman in the White House?"

"Everyone on both coasts goes on welfare. That godless whoremaster Bill Clinton runs wild in the streets, hookers and starlets everywhere. Wall Street tanks. The North Koreans practice dropping nukes on Japan, and the Democrats do nothing but go to peace conferences in Europe at fancy hotels."

POTUS: "As long as they're my hotels."

VP: "Sorry boss, I forgot."

The telephone on the president's desk, the one with the red button, lit up like a stop sign gone mad. The President ignores it but the VP keeps glancing at it.

VP: "Boss, do you want to take the call on the emergency phone?"

POTUS: "Hell no. Hannity is on. I'll pick it up when he's finished."

VP: "It could be important."

POTUS: "More important than Hannity? No way. Probably some general in a shithole country can't find his iPhone and the State Department is having a hissy fit over it. Hold it, I can't say that about his filthy, fly-ridden country. Maybe their dictator choked on his dinner. I hear they eat insects there."

VP: "Is that true, they eat insects in those countries?"

POTUS: "Who gives a shit what they eat. Most of his country is probably starving anyway. Get the phone, Hannity's done."

VP: "Boss, it's your wife, we're late for tonight's reception."

POTUS: "Tell her we'll be there, and tell her to smile for a change."

An aide interrupted the conversation and summoned the two world leaders to the reception. They met their wives in a waiting room off the main ballroom and entered together. As if on cue, they and their wives were all smiling as though they were advertising new teeth on television. They worked their way through the crowded room, accepting compliments, shaking hands, gripping shoulders and elbows, and kissing women on the cheek.

When the president was introduced to Barbara his eyes widened and he looked around to see if his wife was watching him. She was distracted and didn't see him kiss Barbara on the cheek while he slid his hand around to test her flesh, just below her bare shoulder. He looked over the same shoulder and made eye contact with the vice President who silently mouthed the words "Bill Clinton."

The president moved on, after telling Barbara that he hoped she would enjoy dinner and that he would enjoy dinner more if she was seated near him.

After the greet-and-grope had died down, the President summoned the Chief of Protocol and told him to re-arrange the seating chart. Barbara and Eric were moved up the chart to within two place settings of the president. The latter was now able to lean across the ambassador from the impoverished African country with an unpronounceable name, who was the guest of honor, and talk non-stop to Barbara while I hovered silently in the background out of sight.

As they talked, I noticed something odd that had been bothering me. Barbara gave off a delicious scent of fresh fruit that was always present, yet when she was around the president, I could not detect it. There was something present, more powerful, that seemed to nullify the scent I was used to.

Then it came to me. The president had a special odor all his own, powerful and unique; it was something I did not recognize at first, but it was strong, musty, and rank. I was certain it would attract flies since I felt a kind of instinct pulling me toward it, but I resisted. Then came my "aha moment." It was the same smell that I experienced at the race track, that pungent aroma in the stalls, and on the track. Horse manure, of course.

Barbara and the Chief were hitting it off nicely, drawing frowns and grimaces from the First Lady. She warned the newly infatuated president that he had a very busy day tomorrow.

She was well aware that every day was a busy day in the White House, what with dinners, delegations, cabinet meetings, planning sessions, and the crisis de jour. Her insistence led to the President and First Lady's early retirement, but not before invitations were extended to Barbara and Eric by the president to please come back when their film was completed.

The president wished to see it right away, as soon as it was ready for a screening in the White House theater. He added that Reagan was not the only president who loved the movies, he was a big fan too. He especially loved the doomsday films where the White House was blown up. He laughed at his own little joke, the only one to do so that evening.

Barbara nodded politely, but I knew what she was thinking. I would get the proverbial earful later on. Just as Barbara and Eric were about to leave, the evening took an unexpected turn.

The vice president, tight-lipped, solemn, and humorless, motioned them into a sitting room behind an office that I had not explored. He complimented Eric and Barbara on how they had impressed and charmed the president. He had something on his mind other than praise.

VP: "I know I am not popular in Hollywood and neither is the president. We need some friends there and I hope I can count on you two to help us out."

An awkward silence followed.

VP: "We need fundraising help from, what do you people call them, "people in the business." So, I thought I would just ask you some questions to get a feel if you would be the right people."

An even more awkward silence followed.

Eric: "Mr. Vice President."

VP: "Just call me Mike."

Eric: "We're artists, actors, directors and hardly qualified to make political judgments. I have never thought of myself as a political animal, and this takes me by surprise."

VP: "How about you, young lady? Do you have any political views?"

Barbara squirmed in her seat and nearly fell out of her designer gown.

Barbara: "I don't wish to be disrespectful, Mr. Vice President, but I'm strongly opposed to your administration."

VP: "Well, I appreciate your honesty, but what do you really know about it?"

The Vice President's condescending attitude toward her seemed to dissolve Barbara's restraint. That and a little too much wine while fending off the president's undisguised attention loosened her tongue.

Barbara: "Well, Mike, you must think I'm just another dumb blonde, a brainless twit, risen through the ranks of the brainless twits, because of my willingness to have sex with whoever might assist me in the realization of my ambitions. Let me assure you, that is not the case."

VP: "I meant no such thing."

Barbara: "Let me go on. I minored in political science in college and I have continued to read quite a lot on the subjects of immigration, climate change, the continuing war in Afghanistan, the Paris Accords, and other subjects that this president and his administration have mismanaged."

VP: "Tell it to Obama. He's responsible for all these problems."

Barbara: "Not good enough, Mike. You and your boss, together with a spineless Republican Congress, have already set this country back fifty years. "

VP: "I've heard enough young lady. That will be all. This little discussion is over. You may leave now."

The vice president's face was flushed and his expression grim as he summoned security to usher Barbara and Eric out to a waiting limo.

Barbara did not look back, or even attempt civility as she departed. Eric tried in vain to salvage something of the evening by thanking the vice president for his hospitality, but by this time the man was having none of it. Barbara and Eric entered the limo waiting at the White House portico for the short ride to their hotel.

Eric: "For God's sake, Barbara, what were you thinking? That tirade was unbelievable."

Barbara: "That man was the most repulsive, disgusting, smug, self-satisfied..."

Eric cut her off.

Eric: "He's among the most powerful men in the country. People like you and me can't afford to have enemies like that. He could swat us down like flies. He will probably be on Twitter first thing in the morning with the studio heads, or their corporate bosses, telling them we were both drunk and rude to him and the president. I just hope I get my word in first. You can bet there'll be rumors leaked about you and me, that we had sex with the waiters, with each other, or with someone else. Anything and anyone else they can think of to make us look bad. They may even decide to dig up some choice piece of dirt or create it out of whole cloth, and save it for when our film opens in New York."

Barbara wasn't looking so confident anymore.

Barbara: (mumbling): "Eric, you can't be serious. Why would they bother with actors and directors? They need to run the country. They have wars to fight, an economy to manage."

Eric: "They think we mold public opinion. We're fair game. Votes are all they care about. They don't care about the voters themselves."

Barbara wasn't sure if Eric was angry with her or with the criminals in the White House. She half-moaned an apology to Eric and bolted for her room where she dumped me out of her purse on the king-size bed. I scrambled to safety, away from the compact, hairbrush, lipstick, notepad, eyeliner, wallet, and cell phone, any one of which could have maimed me, and nearly did.

Poor Barbara. She was crazed, unable to settle herself. She picked up the house phone, dialed a number, hung up, looked at the phone, and slammed it down again.

She turned on the television, surfed aimlessly with the remote, clicked it off, and threw the remote at the bank of pillows on the bed.

She paced about the suite, threw herself on the bed, sat up, laid down again, and realized she still had on her evening clothes. She threw off the clothes, went into the bathroom, came out with her vibrator, turned it on, turned it off, and threw it against the pillows. She finally noticed me perched on the headboard.

Barbara: "Fly, what have I done? I made a fool of myself, made an enemy for life, and ruined the picture. Eric hates me, the studio could fire both of us; that terrible man will have his goons looking for every piece of dirt he can dig up on me, and God knows I've done some stupid things,

135

everyone has. He's free to murder innocent women and children in the name of peace and freedom. Whose peace and freedom is that?"

Oh, Jesus, why did I ever go to that dinner? I should have shut my big mouth. God, what a fuck-up I am."

I wanted desperately to speak at that moment, to assure Barbara that all was not lost. Perhaps the White House was not so petty that they put revenge at the top of their agenda. Later I learned that revenge and pettiness were the principal characteristics of the administration.

Barbara was guilty of a slightly drunken, liberal outburst at the end of an unusual evening. Lacking a voice, I had to resort to visual aids once again, this time a magazine with an ad for Lunesta. I flew to it and Barbara stared deeply at the page, as though it revealed the truth of the ages.

Barbara: "Sleep, yes, sleep. I have to sleep."

She called room service and asked them to bring up any over-the-counter sedative that they might have for an emergency.

Eric phoned in the late morning to tell her that they would be returning to New York on the afternoon shuttle. Eric reassured her that he had already spoken to the studio and that there would be no repercussions from last night's political indiscretion. The studio bosses were in total sympathy with her remarks, although they would never admit it or have the guts to say those things to the vice president.

After her wake-up call, a bouquet of flowers was delivered to Barbara, along with a note from the president, praising her charm and beauty.

Apparently, there was a division of opinion at the very top level of government.

Chapter 16
The Future

Barbara had regained her composure, at least enough to travel and talk about the upcoming film which was scheduled to begin shooting in New York the following week. Both she and Eric were more than pleased to leave the world of politics behind them.

The film itself was the story of a relationship between Barbara's character, a girl from a small Texas town who had married an Irish New York cop. He was a first responder to the devastation of the Twin Towers in lower Manhattan and lost his life there. At a grief counseling group, she met a light-skinned Creole man from New Orleans, whose wife died during Hurricane Katrina.

Both characters had suffered in the aftermath, trying to rebuild their respective lives. They were torn between memories of their deceased spouses and the demands of families and interrupted careers. Their relationship was colored by the background of the two disasters, which were both personal and national events of great meaning. For Barbara, it was a serious role, far beyond anything she had attempted in her career.

Eric, Barbara, and the remaining cast and crew settled into the somewhat boring routine of making a movie. The endless changes, the rehearsals of new material, the dailies, the many retakes, a stream of decisions by the director and DP over lighting, the close-ups, and the calls from the studio executives. The film plodded forward relentlessly, like a many-legged beast in search of a meal.

Barbara allowed me to see the dailies with her, and it was undeniable that a mood had arisen that the film was certain to be a hit; with top caliber performances, a timely subject, the tragedy and recovery of both New York and New Orleans. It had breadth and scope, and engendered deep personal feelings about the characters, even the minor ones. One of Eric's film critic friends had been allowed to attend the rushes and he was talking industry awards for Barbara. There was a buzz all over New York, with big crowds gathering for the second unit outdoor scenes.

Newspaper and magazine articles were full of news, gossip, and trivia about the film. Eric and his cast of actors and actresses were besieged with requests for interviews and talk show appearances.

Back in LA, the studio executives were already predicting record box office returns. Theatre chains were scrambling to book the picture, publicity, and marketing departments were gearing up, and foreign distributors and sub-distributors were lining up for a piece of the financial pie.

Careers were revived, bonuses were promised, and Wall Street was standing by with revised earnings forecasts for the parent company of the studio. Traders were driving shares higher every week on speculation over record box office, both domestic and foreign.

The memory of the White House dinner was well forgotten, at least by Barbara. The holy grail of Hollywood, a monster hit film, was within reach. A fantasy had arisen that included personal and corporate wealth, cultural impact, awards, and lasting fame. The doorway to a future of continued success loomed large for the principals.

While Barbara nibbled at the fruit of success, I inhaled the sour taste of anonymity. There is a limit to what a fly can do when the person you are most attached to doesn't have the time to meet your needs for companionship, and cannot ever disclose your existence. At home in Malibu, at least I was secure, warm, and comfortable. New York was truly another world, one in which Barbara was at the beck and call of her director, as well as her own drive to succeed. I was more than ready to leave New York.

At last, there was a big wrap party at an expensive New York restaurant. Lots of hugs and kisses. Everyone from the film turned out in their best garb, the husbands and wives of the cast, as well as a hungry group of flies eating the finest garbage North America could offer.

The flies were all strangers to me, the last lot having died off weeks ago. Being in a humble frame of mind, I went out of my way to socialize with the fly population. This time, I found them receptive and willing to interact with me. Something had changed, perhaps my sense of humility and diminished hubris accounted for the acceptance by my own species.

Barbara was radiant, the center of attention at the party. Toasts were made to her, lavish praise bestowed at every turn, future greatness assured. Massive sucking up had begun.

My boredom with the party scene led me to the kitchen, where chaos prevailed amidst rattling pots, sweating cooks, racing waiters, clattering plates, and strident voices. At least there was real action, not the air kisses and the "darling, you look wonderful" and the fussing over clothes and jewelry that seemed to dominate the party.

The kitchen staff and the wait staff were doing a bang-up job of imitating the main room behavior, unseen by the celebrants. Half of the waiters and waitresses were actors so the mimicry came easy. The kitchen people tended to be a little crude and to the point.

A tall blond girl had unbuttoned the top buttons of her blouse to show some cleavage and was vamping the Asian sous chef. The sommelier had assumed the role of studio CEO and was making a five-picture deal with the Latino busboy to play the lead in the next James Bond films. The executive chef, an Austrian, was directing, calling for the elephants, the battle scenes, and, more naked girls. Still, the food poured out of the kitchen in a steady stream.

I was carried away by the frenetic pace, the chatter, the noise, and the contrast with the serene and sophisticated atmosphere of the not-so-real party going on outside the sweaty tempest of the kitchen.

I never saw the near-fatal blow that slammed me up against a stainless steel industrial dishwasher. The teen-age dishwasher had dealt me a glancing blow with a wet dish towel. A reminder that teenage reflexes, sharp as the blade of a Japanese knife, deserved respect.

I slid down the half-soapy exterior of the machine onto the food-encrusted floor. I was stunned, out of breath, not sure if the damage was fatal. I managed to crawl into a space between the wall and the machine, barely avoiding the on-rushing shoe of the boy, now determined to finish the job with a resounding stomp on my body.

One minute a party, the next a funeral. I inventoried my parts to discover that one wing had been partly crushed, one leg dislocated, if not broken and the mid-section of my body badly bruised. My dorsal vessel was pumping like it wanted to burst through my back – yes, flies have a circulatory system but it is an open system where the hemolymph doesn't flow in closed vessels, but bathes my organs directly. I heard a loud whooshing sound, which I soon realized was the dishwasher and not my dorsal vessel. I don't know how long I lay there, hugging the floor, enveloped in the ongoing racket of the kitchen, afraid to move in any direction.

I must have passed out because when I came to, the kitchen was dark and quiet. I lay there for some time, not sure if I could or should move. If the kitchen was closed then the party must be over and Barbara would be gone. Panic set in. She would never find me, and I was unable to fly or walk normally to find her. This was serious.

After several attempts, I managed to fly clumsily onto a counter where I could at least see my surroundings a little better. My damaged left leg hung heavily to one side making my flight unstable. My partly torn left wing beat frantically to keep up with its healthy partner on the right. Reaching the counter took every last bit of my strength and once again I lay exhausted and frightened, face down on a wooden chopping block that smelled of animal meat. Ugh.

By morning, I had regained some of my strength. Flies are much tougher, and more resilient than you might think. My leg would take time to heal, but I could fly slowly, if somewhat awkwardly. Unfortunately, I would be a slow-moving, attractive target, indoors and outdoors, so I needed an escape plan that did not require me to expose myself in my weakened condition.

Morning food deliveries provided me with a plan. The delivery men pushed their crates of vegetables and fruit stacked up on hand dollies and returned to their trucks after the last load. I managed to climb onto the kick-plate of the last hand dolly to leave the restaurant, and rode it onto the back of the delivery van without being noticed.

The van made several stops as it worked its way uptown, giving me time to rest and get my bearings. I was still in pain, but alert enough to go out with a delivery near the Trump Towers, and slide to the sidewalk where I shivered in the cold until I could crawl under the edge of a newsstand.

I would still have to cross several wide streets before I could reach the relative safety of the lobby, and the elevators up to Barbara's apartment, where I could retreat and dream of my life in Malibu.

After several false starts, I hit on the idea of jumping into the trouser cuff of a well-dressed gentleman. He was preoccupied with the morning paper and paid no attention to anything except the paper and the traffic lights. Luckily, he maneuvered straight into the lobby of the Towers, into the elevator, and up to the floor above Barbara. I managed to disentangle myself from his cuff to huddle in the corner of the elevator, but I had to endure endless rides up and down until someone elected to stop on the right floor.

At least I was rested and could scuttle out of the elevator and down the hallway toward what now seemed like the promised land.

At Barbara's door, I went in with room service bringing Barbara a late afternoon snack. It had taken me all day to reach safety, dulled by pain, exhaustion, fear, and hunger. If I had the gift of language, I would have yelled, "Honey, I'm home," or something like that.

I wanted to tell Barbara of my suffering, my courage, my clever escape plan, and my ability to survive under the worst of conditions. I wanted her to comfort me, but first be nearly hysterical with my unexplained absence, mad with grief. She was none of the above. Instead, she was on the phone with her agent, sifting through offers.

Every part of me hurt, but I knew that no help would be forthcoming. Veterinarians don't treat flies. There would be no one to splint my twisted leg, bind my aching ribs, or mend my ravaged wing. Time was my only ally, Barbara my only hope. Ironically, the title of the film that brought Barbara, and me to New York, was "Hope". I would need my share of this ephemeral concept to recover.

Chapter 17
Enter the FBI

Barbara found me the next morning in my usual spot in the pantry. She saw my condition and her initial expression of irritation vanished.

Barbara: "Fly, I couldn't find you at the party, and I thought you went off on your own. I couldn't tell people my pet fly was lost or missing. I was mad at you for disappearing. Maybe you found that disgusting little "Wings" to play with again."

I gave a dismissive buzz. All I wanted was food and rest.

Barbara: "You're hurt, I can see it. Did it happen at the party? One buzz for yes."

She continued to interrogate until she pieced the story together. Then she brought food and drink, murmuring her sympathy and admiration for my escape and return. Days went by in my half-conscious state. I made a point of eating the fermented fruit whenever possible so that I was a little drunk to ease the pain of my wounds. Healing was gradual and not entirely complete. I would fly again, but not as fast, not as confident, and not without effort. My leg would always be a little twisted. The most significant part of my recovery was the time it gave me to question myself, how I fit into Barbara's life, and what I was doing with my own odd existence.

I had always known that my time would be short. I had already exceeded the limits and the odds were still against me, but I never had the feeling that it would end soon.

I had more or less adapted to the (so-called) thought processes of the humans who surrounded me, an understandable inter-species mistake. I reminded myself that I could no longer acquire their attitudes and beliefs, I was on my own. There were no guidelines to follow - and never would be.

What role models did I have? No parents to go to for advice, no well-meaning relatives, no lovers, no counselors, no tutors, no literature -- not even a television show or a movie to depict standards of fly thought and fly behavior. I was sui generis, and that is lonely. I stayed in my funk for weeks, during and after the return to Malibu.

While I wallowed in the shallow pool of self-pity, I failed to notice that the beach in front of the house had been unusually busy. More umbrellas, more men tossing footballs, more traffic in and around the house. There were hard bodies galore, many taking pictures of themselves, their friends, the beach, and the homes alongside the water with their cell phones, and even some high-powered cameras. I gave it no thought, but I should have realized that the weather was not all that good and those playful figures cavorting on the sand and in the water did not belong there.

One early morning, before the fog burned off and before Barbara had finished her breakfast of fruit and cereal, there was a firm knock at the front door on the highway side of the house. Barbara rose unconcerned and proceeded to open the door to confront two tall men, one young, one older, both in dark suits. The latter wore an old-fashioned, out-of-date hat that looked like a prop from a 1950s gangster movie. He displayed a badge and identified himself and his sidekick as FBI special agents from the National Security Branch.

Barbara seemed more puzzled than anything else and invited them into the house and offered them coffee, which they politely refused.

Senior Agent: "We are here on official business," explained the now hatless agent in a polite but formal tone.

Barbara: "Is there something I have done or said that would bring you here?"

Young Agent: "That's what we're here to find out. A grand jury investigation has been opened and we are here to serve you with a subpoena to appear for a hearing. I should also tell you that your house has been under surveillance for the last ten days."

Barbara was stunned by this information. I listened and observed this conversation from the pantry that adjoined the kitchen, where Barbara often spent her mornings. Something in the air interfered with my usual nosiness and kept me in place, away from my normal practice of snooping from a closer vantage point.

Senior Agent: "We would like you to meet with the U.S. Attorney herself, not one of the Assistant U.S. Attorneys, in our downtown office this week before you are asked to testify. You may be a subject of this investigation or merely a person of interest."

Barbara: "What does all this mean?"

Young Agent: "We are not at liberty to discuss this case further, but I can tell you that it involves national security, and the U.S. Attorney only meets with potential defendants on the most important cases."

They handed her the subpoena and left without further explanation. It was all very impersonal and frightening. Barbara had the good sense to run for the phone and call her lawyer, who turned out to be not much help. He supervised her contracts and negotiated deals with producers and studios, yet he had never set foot in a courtroom during his long and profitable career. However, he explained to her that she needed a first-rate criminal defense lawyer and that a grand jury appearance was not to be taken lightly. He would call back with the names of suitable people and would arrange interviews for Barbara. She then called her agent, her manager, her accountant, and one of her friends who worked for a law firm in Santa Monica.

They all assembled in Malibu that evening. Sweating, swearing, and speculating were the order of the day, or more accurately the night. Fear, flat-out fear, was the only thing everyone could agree upon. Her agent was defiant, her manager and her CPA were timid; her accountant wanted to know if she had reported all of her windfall/gambling income to him. Her friend, Wendy, a legal secretary, promised an appointment with a former Assistant U.S. Attorney in her office. This seemed the best alternative for the group.

I thought to myself, "What next, the S.W.A.T. team?"

I went with Barbara in my familiar hiding place the next day to an office on Main Street in Santa Monica. It was an older two-story building that had been tastefully renovated. The place felt immediately comforting to Barbara, who detested the high-rise modernist offices that seemed to house most law firms of any significance. The receptionist, sporting a tasteful ankle tattoo, showed us into a conference room where we met with Albert Freeman, a tall, blond, bearded, soft-spoken man. He seemed sympathetic, yet confident and knowledgeable.

Freeman explained that nothing had yet been filed against Barbara; rather, she appeared to be the subject of an investigation. Whatever facts the U.S. Attorney assembled would be presented to the grand jury, which would either refuse to indict or would, in fact, indict her on the crime charged.

The really bad part, he explained, was that she was not allowed to have a lawyer present when she was questioned before the grand jury and the grand jury always did exactly what the Assistant U.S. Attorney told it to do. A grand jury would indict an alien from outer space for trespassing on our stratosphere if it was presented by the U.S. Attorney's office.

However, if her lawyer could speak to the prosecutor, he could negotiate, and he may discover what crime they believed she had committed. If others were involved, she might testify with immunity; in short, there were several options to explore.

Barbara provided the attorney with the business cards the FBI agents had left with her, wrote him a substantial check, and placed the matter in his hands. That evening the attorney called. He told her the agents were from the National Security Branch of the FBI, which had been formed in September 2005. The mission of this section was twofold; screen and investigate terrorists and find weapons of mass destruction.

Freeman explained that in the past, the FBI confined itself to investigating theft of government secrets and property, money laundering, organized crime, and domestic terrorism. He gave as an example the famous Pentagon Papers case, in which the parties who copied and leaked the government's secret summary of the war in Vietnam were charged with theft and treason, a capital crime, meaning the possibility of a death sentence for the perpetrators of the crime.

Freeman was one of the two defense counsels for the defendants and was familiar with the FBI's tendency to exaggerate. He expressed his skepticism about the current charges.

Barbara: "Albert, please get to the point, what crime have I been charged with, what is this all about?"

Albert: "It seems you were in the White House for a formal dinner some months ago, is that correct?"

Barbara: "Yes, I went with the director of the film I was shooting and met the president and the vice president. I danced with the president and after the party, the vice president took us aside, and we had a rather unpleasant moment with him."

Albert: "Well, exactly how unpleasant was this moment?"

Barbara: "He wanted to know if we would raise campaign funds in the industry, and I told him what I thought about the administration's policies, foreign and domestic."

Albert: "That's it, or is there something more?"

Barbara: "No, that's it. Is it a crime to argue with the vice president?"

Albert: "Well, the FBI thinks that you had some kind of a very small, compact, mobile, remote-controlled camera that you brought into the White House. You infiltrated security and used this device to record extremely sensitive, computerized information in a highly secret location within the White House. They said that this device does not resemble anything they had ever seen before, and it must be an advanced technology they are unfamiliar with."

Barbara: "Incredible. This is absurd, the most fantastic nonsense I've ever heard."

Albert: (persistently) "Wait. They have the device on film from a hidden security camera."

Barbara: (interrupting) "You have to be joking. I did no such thing. I have no spy devices."

Albert: "I haven't finished. They tell me it looks exactly like a fly, a good-sized fly at that."

I was stunned. I thought Barbara might kill me without a second thought. She mumbled to Freeman that she had another call she had to take and would get back to him.

We both knew this would be hard to explain; probably, impossible. Clumsy as the FBI had been, it looked like the secret communication Barbara and I had shared could be exposed. Barbara could be embarrassed, even humiliated.

I could be disposed of. Maybe my fear of the S.W.A.T. team, was not so ridiculous.

Chapter 18
Exposure

Before Barbara was scheduled to appear before the Grand Jury, the FBI showed up at the house again, this time with a total of four agents and large containers to store evidence. They presented a search warrant and Barbara was compelled to allow them to invade her house and her privacy.

Each agent was assigned a section of the house and ordered to find the device that had been caught on film at the White House. Each carried an unflattering, blown-up still photograph of me, hovering over the shoulder of the White House computer nerd.

The agents, all dressed in dark suits and ties, went about their business methodically. They drew room diagrams, sifted through drawers, looked at the undersides of the furniture, took the backs off the radio, the television sets, and the computers, and made notes and drawings as they proceeded. After two hours of this, they convened in Barbara's living room.

The agent who visited the first time, the older man, was in charge of this search.

Lead agent: "Nothing. We've found zip."

A younger agent: "We must have overlooked something."

There was an air of frustration among the group, that grew with the anticipation of returning to the FBI office with nothing in hand.

Third agent: "Wait, did we look at all the kitchen appliances?"

All four moved to the kitchen and went to work. They took apart appliances, removed the trays from the refrigerator, clattered through dishes, bent and twisted to look inside little used shelves and drawers.

They spent fifteen minutes on a complicated wine opener, taking it apart and pointing it around the room as if it would activate something else.

The idea of the remote-controlled device sent them into somewhat of a frenzy. They turned lights on and off in combination with the television and remotes. They changed channels endlessly with the remotes. Then one of the agents had an epiphany. He rushed to the bedroom and brought out Barbara's velvet box.

Barbara: (screaming) "No, no, no! Give that to me. You have no right to do this!"

Naturally, the agents were immediately convinced they had found the missing device. They extracted the shiny silver cylinder from its velvet home and began to wave it around, pointing it at the television, at the toaster oven, and at the computer. Barbara nearly fainted from embarrassment mixed with anger, but recovered enough to scream convincingly.

Barbara: (screaming) "Put that down you fool!"

Third Agent: (Insisting) "This is it. This is it."

Barbara: "It's a vibrator, you idiot. I suppose you've never seen a vibrator in your sheltered life as a government flunky."

Third Agent: (blurting) "Don't get pissy with me, bitch."

The other agents wrestled the vibrator from him and wanted to lock him in the guest closet away from Barbara. The older agent apologized for the younger agent's conduct and sheepishly offered the vibrator back to Barbara, who now took it like a radioactive booby prize.

In the excitement of the moment, I had left my hiding place in the pantry to view the confrontation over the vibrator. I wanted to comfort Barbara, as she was in that vague world between anger and fear. She was shaking, cursing, and sobbing. Four grown men watched her without sympathy.

Older Agent: "Just tell us where it is."

Barbara: "There isn't anything you dummies, you're looking for a fly, a harmless insect."

Fourth Agent: (shouting and pointing) "That's him!"

Maybe I meant for them to see me and bring an end to the harm I had done to Barbara. If they captured me then this ridiculous search for an imaginary device could come to an end. The Grand Jury could go away and Barbara could resume the normal life of a famous movie star, get married to that liar Jeff, or not, buy a bigger house. I just stood in the way; I was the elephant in the room. Better yet, the fly in the ointment.

Lead Agent: "Get him!"

He snatched the vibrator back from Barbara's shaking hands and pointed it at me as he pressed the buttons on the shaft of the instrument. It began to buzz loudly and he shook it as if he expected me to fall to the ground, explode, or react in some mechanically predetermined way. Instead, I flew toward a window, thinking to make my escape, but the ever-alert team of agents beat me to it and closed off my escape route. I flew up to the ceiling and hovered while they debated how to trap me.

One of the agents drew his gun and threatened to shoot me off the ceiling. Barbara resumed screeching and attempted clumsily to get in their way, as they chased me around the room with the drawn gun. They were clearly frustrated but would not give up. I think they call this a Mexican standoff. The gun-toting young agent seemed to be acting like a cowboy, at least the ones I have seen on TV.

Cowboy Agent: (hot-headedly) "Come down or I'll shoot you down."

Another agent had gone for the television remote, so one was waving a gun, the other was clicking the TV remote at me, and the agent in charge was thrusting the vibrator vigorously toward me. I wish a video could have been made of this scrum. Agent Four was busy taking notes and would have been better served using his iPhone to record this mess.

I remained at ceiling level, looking desperately for another exit strategy. The guy with the gun was scary, so much so that he frightened his fellow agents. Their cries and instructions to put down the gun did nothing but inflame him. He swiveled the gun, pointing it at me as I searched for that elusive path to safety.

Lead Agent: (shouting) "Cut that cowboy shit and give me your gun."

No answer. The cowboy agent was jumping at me, with his gun extended to get a close-up shot. I gave up on finding a way out and conceived a different plan. If I didn't want to be shot, I would attach myself to a bulletproof target.

I flew down from the ceiling and landed on the lead agent's hair, assuming that the cowboy was not so crazy that he would shoot his boss in the head to get at me. This entire rumble began to look like a Marx Brothers comedy skit with me playing Harpo, the ever-silent brother.

The young agent pointed his gun reflexively, at the lead agent's head, then realized what he had done and brought it to his side. His three fellow agents disarmed him and forced him into a sitting position on the living room couch.

I wasn't home free, because my accusers began to swat at me. I escaped once again to the ceiling, but this time the agents stood on chairs, wielding rolled-up magazines, and came after me while Barbara milled about shouting profanities.

I went back to the top dog's head again, knowing it would enrage and provoke them. I didn't foresee that the two lesser agents would attack the boss with rolled-up magazines, so this strategy was abandoned, but not before the head man nearly ripped these two guys a new one; at least that's the expression I heard on re-runs of Law and Order when the top cop decided to embarrass one of his underlings.

This dance could have gone on for hours, as there was no way they could trap me on the ceiling. More for diversion and time to think, I flew into the different rooms in the house. The agents scrambled madly to keep up with me. I even flew into the bathrooms, where they fell all over themselves and crowded in to stand on the toilet, waving towels, and throwing rolls of toilet paper at me. I was wearing them out, but wrecking Barbara's house in the process.

After a time, they gave chase one at a time, while the others took a breather and plotted strategy. In Barbara's den, there was a shelf seven feet up from the floor on which she had Indian baskets and pots displayed. It was there, out of sight of the agents, that I chose to rest. The agent on my tail grabbed a chair and stood on it. He took down each pot and bowl, and I had to then vacate my temporary shelter. We eyed each other with mutual hatred, he standing on a chair, and me backing away toward the rear of the shelf.

Agent: (shouting) "He's trapped, I've got him trapped."

Barbara rushed into the room ahead of the other agents.

Barbara: (crying) "Leave him alone! He's done nothing to you!"

She had reacted without thinking, and the agents caught her error. They had her surrounded in the small den, and she looked from face to face as they silently nodded to one another.

Lead Agent: "So, what's going on with you and this fly?"

Barbara shook her head back and forth but didn't speak. They interrogated her for half an hour with questions she would not answer, other than to deny that I was a mechanical device or that she controlled me in some fashion. Then they huddled alone and afterward announced to her that if she didn't come clean with her story, they would seal off the house and spray poison gas into the den to kill me, after which they would do an autopsy and find out if there was a chip of some kind implanted in my body that allowed her to control me.

It certainly looked like the end for me and the beginning of a difficult, if not impossible explanation for Barbara. I decided then that it was time to end this craziness, give myself up, and take the heat off Barbara. Let them do with me what they will. I flew off the ledge and landed on Barbara's shoulder. The agents rushed at her and she recoiled.

Barbara: (screaming while holding her arms out to protect me) "Don't touch me you, bastards!"

I then flew and landed on the head agent's lapel, on top of his American flag pin.

Agent: "He's giving up, the son of a bitch knows what he's doing!"

Barbara was in tears.

Barbara: "What will you do with him?"

Lead Agent: "Damned if I know. He's the one in the picture, so we bring him in and let the higher-ups figure this one out. Time for the fly to lawyer up."

Chapter 19
Authority

Barbara agreed to go downtown with me to greet my fate, whatever it was. Lacking a proper container, I rode in my usual place in Barbara's purse, although the agents insisted on carrying the purse. I had time to reflect on what lay ahead. They could not put me in jail unless they retrofitted a cell. They would have a hard time explaining me to the other people in the lockup. They couldn't charge me with a crime; no laws are written for insects. What they could do was study me, meaning that if they found nothing the next step would be dissection. They would murder me in the name of science.

I ended up on the desk of the U.S. Attorney for the Central District of California. She was flanked by the FBI Special Agent in Charge of the Southern California Office, and a professor of entomology from the University of Southern California. The professor wanted to pin me to a specimen pad and get up close with his magnifying glass. The FBI agent wanted to match me to the photograph and the U.S. Attorney insisted on reading my rights to me.

Barbara had summoned her lawyer to protect her interests, so everyone had an agenda but no idea how to proceed. The first question was whether a mechanical device was hidden somewhere on my body. Barbara asked whether an X-ray or an MRI would disclose it and if it would do any physical damage to me. Nobody knew the answer to that question, flies never having been x-rayed or subjected to an MRI to the best of anyone's knowledge.

Barbara's lawyer argued that the FBI had found nothing in her house to reveal any kind of a device and no evidence of recordings or data. At this point, I thought I might impress someone if I hummed and buzzed the 'Star Spangled Banner' to prove that I was a patriotic American fly. Bad idea. I rightly sensed that humor has no place in legal proceedings.

Someone had the bright idea to ask Barbara if she communicated with me. She had been dreading the question, and she hesitated, but finally acknowledged that she did. She decided on a demonstration, telling me to fly across the room and land on the telephone, then move to the computer, and then return to the conference table. I followed instructions, and upon landing, I was met with dead silence in the room.

Barbara: (muttering) "Well, we can do this over and over and you cannot deny that he understands us. If you think it's just me, Professor you give him some instructions."

The professor had me go from the floor to the ceiling; I crawled, I flew, I did figure eights, and I did what he told me to do until he was satisfied that he had been understood. Barbara put me through the buzzing routine, one buzz yes, two buzzes no. The others asked the questions and I gave the answers. Everyone wrote furiously on their notepads and iPads.

The U.S. Attorney, a brisk, efficient woman wearing a dark blue power suit that matched her icy blue eyes, directed everyone to abandon the conference table and take seats on her leather couch and deep leather chairs. She spoke calmly to the assembled group.

U.S. Attorney: "Nothing we saw or heard today must ever leave this room. There must be no press, no leaks, no publicity, no rumor, not a hint of this unexplainable phenomenon."

Professor: (protesting) "But this must be explained, it must be studied in the interest of science."

U.S. Attorney: "I agree that it must be investigated, but very carefully and very quietly under my control. For one thing, if any media gets a hold of this story, every one of us could be ruined, with our credibility irreparably damaged. Secondly, our government could become the laughingstock of the world, talking to insects for starters. I hesitate to even approach my superiors with this information, and I will not do so until I have thought through the ramifications of this discovery.

There will be no Grand Jury investigation or hearing in this matter. I will dismiss this present Grand Jury without delay. The fly will be under my personal custody. I want each of you to surrender all notes you took today and I want your cell phones, all of them. As far as I am concerned, this meeting never took place and each of you should remember only that you have forgotten everything that never happened here."

There was dead silence in the room. When all the phones and notes had been collected by Mrs. Olson, she continued to stare at us before adding to her remarks.

U.S. Attorney: "I must also ask each of you individually to assure me that you will not discuss this meeting and its subject matter, the fly, with any third party, meaning wives, husbands, friends, children, relatives, reporters, publishers, dates, or any third parties.

She started for the door, but then with her hand still on the door handle, she turned and spoke again.

U.S. Attorney: "I neglected to tell you that if I should ever learn that you disregarded my instructions concerning this peculiar fly, I will see to it that each of you will be prosecuted to the full extent of the law. I will initiate a Grand Jury proceeding to indict you for lying to a federal law enforcement official and possibly other federal crimes like sedition, conspiracy, treason, and whatever is appropriate to the circumstances under which you violated my trust in you to maintain this secret as a matter of national security."

She then opened the door, and I glimpsed the three additional FBI agents who ransacked Barbara's home seated side by side in the waiting area, grinning at the images on the Cowboy Agent's smartphone.

I flew quickly over their heads as the meeting disbanded and all except Barbara headed for the elevators. I observed the three junior agents watching a porn video. The male figure in the video was Adam. I would keep this to myself.

These agents wouldn't be laughing and smiling after Mrs. Olson finished with them. I was none too happy myself as I flew back to be with Barbara. I had met my new mistress and life would be very different from now on. Of course, anybody after Barbara was a demotion; more like a disappointing blind date that turns into an arranged marriage in a jurisdiction that prohibits divorce.

Chapter 20
Captivity

The U.S. Attorney, Mrs. Olson, having dismissed the others, kept Barbara back for a personal conversation before she dealt with the giggling FBI agents. She asked Barbara to surrender her custom purse so that I could be hidden and would also feel more comfortable. She seemed to warm up to Barbara and became sympathetic.

Mrs. Olson: "My dear, I know this must be difficult for you; it's such an odd situation as there is no one to talk to or share it with you. Have you ever spoken to anyone about him, or it, or whatever you call him?"

Barbara. "I just call him Fly and I never had the guts to tell anyone, although my boyfriend had suspicions."

Mrs. Olson: "I can't believe I am having a conversation with you about an insect who understands and communicates with us."

Barbara nodded and then said something that shocked me.

Barbara: "Mrs. Olson, it is truly a burden to be aware of something in the universe that no one else can accept. I didn't ask for and didn't want this; what is it, a relationship? I don't like bugs, snakes, or insects in general; I especially don't like flies and here I am trying to hold off the

FBI; being hauled up to face a grand jury; my home violated and trashed; and, all because of a fly that I fed and cared for because he attached himself to me. I can now go back to my work and this secret I had to keep at all costs is now yours."

I could hardly believe what I was hearing. Did I attach myself to her? Of course, she encouraged me and used me. Did she forget about going to the track, the stock killing she made because of me, the monster bet in Las Vegas, and all the tidbits of information she used to her benefit?

I was being dismissed without so much as a thank you, not a moist eye, not a pang of regret, not a little shiver of the heart. Merely a burden lifted. Nothing remembered of those special moments we shared.

How about when she told me she wished I was a guy and she would show me a night that I would never forget? It looks like she forgot it all.

I treasured every day with her, every triumph over a world that would never accept me. We were intimate in our way; would she tell Mrs. Olson how she let me linger on her body, drink in her delicious odor, share in her arousal? I don't think so.

I should have known that the human propensity to act for one's own benefit transcends religion, morals, the social contract, and the bonds of friendship and family. It is a law of nature. Situational ethics is a term I heard of, but never saw it directly applied. Now I know what it means. Me first, everyone else, you're on your own. Mere loyalty and devotion earn a few points, but at crunch time, if you have to kick someone else to the curb to save yourself, don't hesitate.

Had I been able to shed tears, I would have drenched the room.

Barbara started to leave.

Barbara: "He needs a steady diet of fresh fruit, and of course, you will want to keep him out of sight. There isn't much more to tell, so good luck with whatever you decide to do with him."

I chose to believe that Barbara was embarrassed to admit that she had feelings about me. She didn't want this formidable woman, an important government official, to know the depth of her feelings. Perhaps I rationalized this for my own benefit. People often did this when the truth was too bitter to accept.

This was a test of my self-esteem. If I believed in myself, I could explain and accept her behavior. Otherwise, I would be crushed, knowing that all along our relationship meant nothing to her. I was a burden to be disposed of at the first opportunity.

I did present some problems for her, and with the FBI at her doorstep maybe she chose her own survival to that of an insignificant fly.

There must have been a lesson for her in the experience; she was beautiful, a movie star, young, smart, rich, desirable, and famous. But not bulletproof. Not even the president of the nation, that goofy, odd-smelling, makeup-encrusted, con artist is above the law.

Without further ceremony, I was carted off, a casualty of my own bravado. No more roaming about hotels, restaurants, parties, boardrooms, and bedrooms. I was a marked fly. For me, it was a high-rise condo in downtown LA; lots of glass, sparsely decorated in neutral colors, angular furniture covered in some sort of abrasive microfiber, no television playing, no visitors. It was a purely functional, sterile living space in keeping with the demeanor of the only inhabitant, the stern, efficient, dedicated Mrs. Olson.

She was a Republican appointee, rescued from an obscure, federal regulatory agency, with something to do with agriculture, and stuffed into the U.S. Attorney's office over the silent protest of the career lawyers serving there. She was determined to prove her worth through sheer efficiency.

Mrs. Olson frowned upon entertainment, amusement, conversation, or relationships. She was a Calvinist, descended from the pilgrims, completely out of touch with current society. From my limited understanding, she was not so different from the majority of the Supreme Court justices.

There was a Mr. Olson, a lobbyist in Washington for the pork industry, who made a rare phone call, never visited, but occasionally sent flowers or candy. The arrangement seemed to suit Mrs. Olson; she had little time to squander on her husband, or me. It meant solitary confinement.

This went on for months, until I determined to do something about my state of affairs. I kept hoping that Barbara would find some excuse to see me, even take me out of the condo on the twenty-first floor for a few hours, but it was not to be. After a few months that fantasy died away, and I was ready to make my move.

I began by hanging around my keeper whenever she was in the condo. I made it personal by slipping into the bathroom when she was showering, relieving herself, making up her face, and picking out her clothing for the day, even though every outfit in her closet had the same antiseptic, off-the-rack Walmart look. She noticed and initially sneered at me, but I kept it up.

Soon she was slamming doors on me, scowling at my presence, even talking to me in that commanding, authoritarian voice usually reserved for underlings, ordering me back to my corner in the pantry. She would have put a dunce cap on me if it was possible.

At least she was paying some attention to me. She knew I was up to something, but she wasn't sure just what. My plan was simple; she would tire of me and get rid of me. When in doubt about a problem give it to someone else. As a government lawyer, she had to know this; it's what Congress does on a regular basis.

There was risk involved, not knowing who that next person might be or what that person would do with me. I did consider that I might be shipped off to the entomology department at USC for study, dissection, and embalming. In fact, that was exactly what Mrs. Olson decided to do with me. She could see no useful purpose for me to remain in her custody, and she could not find a way to solve the dilemma I presented to her. Better disappearance than disorder.

Then one rainy weekend day, when she was not running off to her office and had nothing to do but stay home and be irritated by my presence things came to a head.

Mrs. Olson: "You serve no useful purpose, either to me or to mankind. If someone should discover that I am keeping you or talking to you I could be labeled as a head case, a nut case, an alien, or a communist, anything at all."

"At first, I thought I could explain this to our government if I had time to observe you. I would make some important use of your talents, as did your prior owner, but now I see that is impossible. You are lazy, shiftless incorrigible, and nothing but a mutant insect. No one will notice or miss your passing in the least. I would do away with you myself, but Professor Barnes thinks that you must be examined and dissected in the name of science. Now get into this jar and be quick about it."

She held out a glass jar, the size of a drinking glass with a paper top, into which several holes had been crudely poked. I refused to follow orders to leap into this insect's coffin. Instead, I flew high onto a glass window out of her reach and watched the rain beat down on the city.

Mrs. Olson: "I am warning you, fly. I will move to a hotel and have this place sprayed with lethal gas every day until they remove you, dead, drugged, and done for."

I didn't move until she got out her iPhone and began calling exterminators. She made a date for the following Tuesday, but when she hung up the phone, I was parked at the bottom of the hideous glass jar.

Chapter 21
New Assignment

My new home was to be in a lab building at USC, a low-rise structure that butts up against the 110 Freeway. There were specimens everywhere, and not just flies. There were containers of every size and shape, like mini apartment houses filled with insects. Food, if you could call it that, and water to sustain the prisoners were in short supply. It was an insect gulag, a way station on the journey to the great beyond. Microscopes, dissecting tables, Bunsen burners were the furnishings. Assistants in stained white coats shuffled back and forth with their small instruments of torture.

The loud buzzing noise of the flies, like the vuvuzelas at a soccer match, filled the room. It was a collective voice of sheer terror, a wordless plea to be let loose.

Professor Barnes was delighted to see me. He was salivating. He picked up my jar and took me to his private office, a cubby hole with steel gray furniture and specimens too numerous to count, displayed on whiteboards with Latin names printed underneath the unfortunate victims of his research.

I thought of the Viet Nam memorial in Washington DC which honored the American service persons who died in that sorry war.

There could never be a memorial for all the insects who perished at the hands of Professor Barnes. It would take too many acres of land and full-sized buildings to house that memorial.

Immediately, the phone rang, and Barnes engaged in a heated conversation that involved me. I recognized the voice of the FBI agent who led the search of Barbara's house to arrest me.

Agent: "Dr. Barnes, that fly you inherited from Mrs. Olson now belongs to me. I should say he belongs to the FBI and I am coming by your office to pick him up today. Do not run tests on the fly, do not do anything that might disturb his unique abilities."

Barnes: "This is outrageous. This mutant insect represents an unheard-of phenomenon that only further scientific study can explain. I need to test his intelligence, open up his brain, and perhaps breed him to another insect. This is a once-in-a-lifetime scientific opportunity. What does his DNA contain that resulted in this mutation?"

Agent: "The FBI has an immediate use for this fly. His ability to bring back critical information cannot be overestimated or delayed. I will be at your office in half an hour to pick him up. If he has been damaged, or if he is unable to follow instructions, you will be held responsible."

Barnes: "Responsible for what? The death of an insect? I'm calling the President of this

University to intervene. You are not welcome here because you have no understanding of the importance of this discovery. I am saving him, while you will destroy him on some capricious, meaningless enterprise that will pale in comparison to his importance to science."

Agent: "This fly will be placed in the hands of an informant in Mexico. He can supply us with information about the drug cartels that are murdering hundreds of people in the US, Mexico, Europe, and Asia. We can save untold numbers of innocent people who deserve to live. We can shut down the drug trade with his help, free up law enforcement to deal with immigration, gun violence, and the social cost of these problems."

Barnes: "I'm not giving this Fly to you without a fight. He means too much to entomology. You want to toss him into the cesspool of the drug world where he might catch a few unimportant criminals. If science can explain his ability to communicate with humans, it changes the world as we know it. I would probably win a Nobel prize for that achievement and you want to hand him over to Mexican drug agents! Fuck the FBI!"

Barnes slammed the phone hard enough to shake the table that held the container designed by Mrs. Olson, which now resided on a shaky metal table. My immediate concern was to survive a shower of glass shards likely to imbed themselves in my unprotected body if the jar fell to the floor. Fortunately, the insect coffin righted itself, and I was spared once again.

The FBI agent, Johnny Ray Jones, showed up promptly and muscled straight into Barnes' lab without knocking on the door or announcing his presence. He quickly identified where I was held, lifted the container, and stuck it into a paper shopping bag. There was no further discussion with Professor Barnes, who was helpless to stop the agent. Johnny Ray never even took off his standard FBI hat, usually part of FBI protocol.

Agent: "This is now government property. Do not interfere. I am armed and authorized by the U.S. Attorney for the Southern District of California and the Special Agent in Charge of the FBI Office in Los Angeles to take possession of this container and its occupant."

Barnes called the University President, who was engulfed at the moment by scandals. Recruiting of football players using hookers as bait, and lawsuits against the university for medical staff's sexual improprieties were just a few of the problems du jour. There was no time for her to listen to stories from Barnes about gifted insects.

We proceeded to the agent's parked car and drove to his condo in Pasadena instead of the FBI office downtown. It was nothing like Malibu but it definitely beat Mrs. Olson's glass-walled tower of sterility.

Johnny Ray let me out of the container and took a fruit plate from his refrigerator which I jumped on.

Agent: "You can thank your girlfriend for this fruit. She also gave me the idea that you could go to work for the FBI. I'm going to hand you over to an informant I control in Mexico who is planted in a violent narco-terrorist gang in a remote section of that country. "

"You can give us information about drug routes, shipment dates, and smuggling in and out of Mexico. If we had that information, we could shut down the source of their money, which they can't do without. You just might bring down the biggest source of illegal drugs in the world, stop the gang wars, the assassinations, the kidnappings, even the corpse messaging."

Maybe he should have asked me to solve the problems of world hunger, or world peace. My chances of accomplishing the impossible tasks he set for me had no limits. My immediate issue was survival. The choice was spying vs. dissection, an easy decision for me to make, although others were making it for me.

The high point of my stay in Pasadena was the television coverage of the premiere of Barbara's film made in New York. Her entry onto the red carpet would be talked about for years. Her appearance on the red carpet for the obligatory interview in advance of the first public screening of the film was dramatic itself.

She was escorted by the two black men, each seven feet tall, one on each arm. Her gloved right arm was held by the young Laker player whom she had dated since she returned from New York.

On the other side was the owner of the truck Jeff had damaged and fled from. Both of these giants were dressed in perfectly tailored black tuxedos, highlighted by gold Laker basketball shoes. They were an instant hit with the frenzied crowd, packed in the bleachers on each side of the red carpet. The fans threatened to breach the erected barriers and rush en masse into the entry to the theatre.

Barbara, elegant in a simple off-the-shoulder black evening dress, with no jewelry except a simple string of pearls, remained calm in the eye of the pandemonium she had created. She was interviewed as expected, yet managed to rise above the banal and insipid conversations that usually mark these publicity events.

She spoke briefly about the film's generosity of spirit, and the humanity shown by people in the wake of disasters, both natural and deliberate. She then introduced her escorts as men of integrity and purpose whom she invited to escort her to this special event.

She maintained her dignity amid the artificial pomp and circumstance generated by the studio's publicity department and was rewarded with a massive cheer and applause from the crowd as she entered and again when she finished her interview. Even Johnny Ray shouted his approval at the television set.

I learned that Barbara pursued this agent, Johnny Ray, after my discovery. She told him how I gathered information from the neighbors in Malibu, from the jockeys at the racetrack, and from the bettors in Vegas. She told him how to communicate with me and what I was capable of doing for the FBI.

She sold him on the opportunity to make a name for himself in the FBI that would jump him over his rivals for advancement in the hierarchy of the organization, maybe even beyond. He could take all the credit, receive the pay raises, collect the medals and the honors, and share them with no one. He bought into it. He had nothing to lose, and if anyone ever suggested that a fly on the wall had provided the information, he would laugh at them. Perfect deniability, he called it.

As a bonus, Barbara hooked Johnny Ray up with her talent agency, and they found Johnny Ray some consulting work on crime shows and movies that led to him taking character parts in both worlds. Between his FBI job and the extra side hustle, he was living a more interesting life and making far more money than he had ever seen in his adult life. And, he loved hanging out with her. Who wouldn't?

There were a few details to work out before I shipped out for Mexico. Johnny Ray was not about to tell some lowly informant that the FBI, the most venerated name in the world of law enforcement, was communicating with, and relying upon, a not-so-common fruit fly for information. This would not strike fear in the hearts of the narco-terrorists.

My handler would be told that I was a recording device, perhaps the most sophisticated piece of compact machinery ever devised by man. I emitted signals to a satellite that returned audiovisuals in real-time, and none of it could be detected, jammed, copied, or hacked.

Other than being holed up with the nastiest thugs on the planet, my biggest concern was food. I would have to provide for myself with whatever slop these sub-human killers and drug traffickers left on their plates or in their garbage. There would be no Gelson's takeout or cups of fresh fruit with yogurt lying about, presented to me on sparkling clean china.

If they noticed me or caught me, I would be extinguished, executed not as a dangerous spy for the FBI but merely dispatched as vermin. There would be no dramatic show trial, no hue and cry in the media to save the brave young fly who dared to go amongst these monsters and bring them down for the love of country. There would be no drawn-out diplomatic bargaining for my release, not even a casket draped in a flag while hundreds lined up to mourn my passing.

More to the point, it was Mexico or the dissection table.

I made the obvious choice and silently thanked Barbara, my patron saint, who made it possible. She had not forgotten me, only devised a plan to save my sorry insect carcass.

Chapter 22
Mexico

I was fully briefed before being deposited into the vortex of chaos, murder, revenge, and political resistance brewing in the cities of Michoacán. Johnny Ray would personally transport me across the border in a tricked-out FBI van. It had the electronics of Air Force One, and the weaponry of a modern infantry battalion. Johnny Ray had direct feeds to the Pentagon, FBI headquarters, the Justice Department, the DEA, the CIA, and his Hollywood agent.

We flew commercial to San Antonio and picked up the FBI van. From there, it was down the east coast of Mexico, with a lot of slow going on one-lane roads with their fair share of potholes until we headed inland to Morelia, and met with our informant, in what appeared to be an abandoned warehouse in a seedy, grimy part of town. After days of travel, the van and its two inhabitants blended seamlessly into the landscape of dust, dirt, and drab.

Johnny Ray talked through the whole trip when he wasn't listening to country music. It didn't matter that I couldn't talk back; he had an audience and needed no more. Now and then he let me out of the container to get a little exercise flying around the van in small towns where we stopped for water, food, and gas.

He went on and on about the leader of the Los Proscritos cartel (Spanish for The Outlaws). El Brazo Fuerte (Spanish for The Strong Arm) was already a mythical figure in Mexico.

El Brazo was reputedly smart, cruel, religious, and a man of honor, not merely a greedy gangster. He threw lavish parties and gave money generously to the poor and to widows, some of whom he created, in his fiefdom. He had a thriving network of methamphetamine labs and real estate holdings as well, like men's clubs, mini-malls, bars, and restaurants. He stood openly against the Federales, Mexico's famously corrupt federal army troops, and against the local police departments who were even more corrupt.

According to Johnny Ray, El Brazo began his career by kidnapping important government officials, high-ranking foreign diplomats, wives and children of Mexican billionaires, and even famous racehorses. He then demanded and received vast amounts of money, assets, and gold.

Other times he obtained state secrets, which he sold back to their source. With the ransom monies, he funded the gang's recruitment of members and the purchase of haciendas, safe houses, and other businesses he deemed important and useful to his empire.

El Brazo's success in rural, and then urban, areas of Michoacán, led him to expand into other Mexican states, at the expense of the local homegrown cartels. They were no match for El Brazo and his legions, fueled by money and religion.

In a relatively short time, El Brazo shifted away from kidnapping and into drugs as he looked northward to the US and the insatiable demand of its residents for drugs of every flavor.

According to the FBI, Los Proscritos had muscled into major drug activity in the nearby states of Guerrero, Morelos, Guanajuato, Colima, and Jalisco and was threatening Sinaloa, the coastal state, long the center of the Mexican drug trade. Rumor had it that this backwoods cartel had developed sources in China, India, Bulgaria, and Holland for meth production and distribution. These were small-town mountain boys who gouged out a place in the world, led by a charismatic folk hero.

At the warehouse in Morelia, I was handed over to the "mole," as Johnny Ray called him. He was instructed not to tamper with my "controls" and once again told that I was the most sophisticated device the FBI had ever developed for eavesdropping. A fortune equivalent to the cost of an aircraft carrier had been spent on developing and disguising the device as a common fruit fly, and I would exhibit every characteristic of a fly at all times.

Under no circumstance should he treat me as anything but an ordinary fly. I would be recording everything that went on within Los Proscritos' headquarters for the next week or more if necessary. If there was some malfunction, the mole would be notified to pick me up and return me to Johnny Ray, who would be conveniently vacationing in Acapulco among the rich gringos. I would be returned to this same warehouse in Morelia in the same container that now held me.

The mole, Juan, was a Mexican man in his early thirties, dressed in rough peasant clothing. He had been a policeman in San Antonio when the FBI recruited him for training in undercover work. He was selected for the Michoacán assignment because he had family in the Tierra Caliente region, where there was a historical streak of anti-government sentiment. He was of medium height, with thick black hair and a trim goatee. He seemed to take his instructions seriously and handled my containment jar with great care, as if I was nuclear waste.

We made our way in Juan's run-down pickup truck to a mountain town in the west part of Michoacán. It was called Apatzingán, very pretty and quiet, nestled in the mountains. The mole's primary responsibility was the delivery of food to Los Proscrito's hacienda on the outskirts of town. Sometimes it was prepared by vendors in town, and other times he brought dressed meats to be hung in a large freezer, for butchering on-site for big parties and events.

He was allowed to occasionally eat with the gang members, hang around and drink beer, and generally participate in the news and gossip about the goings on in town and other places of interest to the gang. The big occasions were when El Brazo and his entourage were in residence. He had several haciendas in the territories he controlled and his security lay in the constant, unpredictable movement between these haciendas and other safe houses.

Apatzingán was an important strategic location for several reasons. It was not too distant from the port city of Lazaro Cardenas, where drug shipments came in from Central and South America. The mountain terrain provided cover for the many meth labs owned and run by the gang. And it was close to the hidden mountain valleys where opium poppies were grown, harvested, and processed for shipment to the U.S.

To my great surprise, the hacienda outside the village was fruit fly heaven. The hacienda windows and doors were always open to the warm, soft breezes and the scent of flowers growing everywhere. Fruit was fresh and plentiful. Homegrown fruit that I had never heard of, or seen, was everywhere. Dragon fruit, zapote, rambutan, and cherimoya to name just a few. There was familiar fruit like mango, papaya, and guava. It was sweet tasting and never refrigerated to blunt the taste in the name of preservation. It was eaten by the constant flow of men and women in the hacienda or thrown away as garbage. A vast army of flies dined daily on this delicious food.

Given the endless supply of fruit, the flies were not in fierce competition for nutrition. The overall environment was upbeat and friendly among the flies and the humans. People and flies circulated through the many rooms of the hacienda without much restriction or privacy, except for the one or two bedrooms reserved for El Brazo. Nobody was much interested in the flies, they were merely part of the background, not hunted, despised, or vilified.

I was careful to be social with my own species so as not to stand out. Food was our common bond, as it is everywhere, and so I managed to integrate myself into the daily routine without incident. I wandered about the hacienda into the meeting rooms, bedrooms, library, and chapel.

There was a strong religious element in Los Proscritos, with prayer meetings and book groups to instruct and motivate the faithful. This strong religious element drew upon an evangelical U.S.-based Christian cult that preached a doctrine of purification by violence, if necessary and forgiveness by a tolerant, benign God. Every gang member carried his own paperback copy of the philosophy, and time was reserved each day to either read or receive instruction from senior gang members.

The many television sets in the hacienda were on non-stop. Gang members often watched the religious shows and the telenovelas while cleaning, fondling or loading their pistols and rifles. Occasionally there would be talk of violence, even murder, when necessary to accomplish an important gang mission, after which the active participants would vacation in Apatzingán to cool out.

The religious messages served to justify the violence and soothe the conscience of the gang members directly involved. The Bible, as it turns out, is replete with violence, even though it says the meek shall inherit the earth. Los Proscritos dogma clearly states that the meek shall not inherit the earth, or anything else.

The only positive part of the Los Proscritos social and political platform that distinguished them from the other bloodletting cartels was the choice never to kill women.

They might be treated as servants, inferiors, beaten, abused, and sexually exploited, but they were still mothers and sisters, and were valued as caregivers, and providers of beauty, warmth, and devotion to men. They were exempt from extreme violence. That same kindness would not extend to flies.

Chapter 23
El Brazo

El Brazo arrived after I had been there for almost a week. A grand fiesta was planned in his honor. He arrived in a caravan of black Audi SUVs, the favored vehicle of narco-terrorists.

He looked pretty much like everyone else; stocky, late thirties, tattooed, mustachioed, acne scars on his cheeks, but with a definite presence. He wore no flashy jewelry, just the obligatory crucifix, T-shirts, jeans, and long black hair; he could have passed for just another gangbanger.

His name, El Brazo Fuerte, had something to do with the strong-arm role he had played in the gang on his way to the leadership role he now occupied. He sported pumped-up biceps from years of bodybuilding in prison, hence the name El Brazo was earned and adopted. He looked and played the role of the smoldering religious avenger, unbound by any rules but his own.

The celebratory fiesta to welcome El Brazo accorded with my expectations. Whole roasted pigs, baskets of fresh shrimp from the coast, non-stop dancing, tequila swigging, pistols fired into the night air, pretty girls, and clouds of marijuana smoke. The fly population went crazy right along with Los Proscritos, sopping up the leftovers, relieved from the pursuit of trash for one night.

The celebration went on late into the night until El Brazo called for a next day noon meeting in the library, then retired to his private suite, staffed by a local girl of his choice.

The library meeting was for higher-ups in the gang's food chain. After the night of revelry, it was all business in the daytime. Large topographical maps of the Tierra Caliente area and the Sinaloa coastline were laid out on a huge library table. There were tide change tables, water depth charts, and photographs of various landing crafts. The meth labs and roads leading to Morelia were shown on a map of their own. Unfortunately for me, all the debates over these strategic items were in Spanish. I never learned Spanish and could make little sense of the discussions.

The FBI failed to consider this negative factor when it drafted me into its service.

I could not be positive, but I learned a few things. It looked like Los Proscritos was bringing in a huge shipment of cocaine from South America and would land it on the beach below Lazaro Cardenas. At the same moment, they would create a diversion in the port city that would draw the attention of the local and federal police. They would appear to be caught shipping marijuana in big cargo containers and the police would think they had made a major drug bust.

The "marijuana" would be roots, twigs, bark and other harmless stuff to add weight and bulk to the shipment. Of course, many of the local law enforcement officers were on Los Proscritos' payroll and would play along with the charade, while the real action was down the coast. The real drug shipment would be raced on shore by a fleet of power boats, then taken overland to one of the larger meth labs controlled by the gang.

When the meeting broke up for lunch, food and drink were served on the outside patio. I was able to get closer to the maps, where important elements were marked by red pencils. The markings were of labs and buildings hidden in the small mountain towns on the road to Morelia, as well as roads leading to and from Lazaro Cardenas. I memorized everything.

The afternoon session in the library shifted to something entirely different. An older woman, wearing peasant clothing, was shown into the space with a bag full of tacos. She disclosed the contents to the men, then measured out a handful of white powder from a container, poured it into a plastic baggie, sealed it, and inserted the baggie into the taco where she covered it with lettuce and other ingredients. The men laughed and joked about the tacos and experimented with them, mimicking the instructor.

El Brazo spoke after the demonstration, gesturing, pointing at the labs, the bay, the photos, and the roads. He then launched into a speech holding the paperback book that all his followers already possessed. He used the word

Dios over and over. His right arm shot up with his right hand clenched in a fist as he repeatedly made his point, followed by "Dios Lo Quiero!"

He and Dios seemed to be on the same page. His followers shouted their approval, burst from the room onto the patio, and fired their weapons to the apparent delight of El Brazo. The library was deserted during the evening meal and the drinking that followed.

Everything from the day's meeting was left on the library table. As I looked for more clues, I noticed a slight residue of white powder on the table left from the demonstration conducted by the older woman. I flew down to it and tasted it to see if it was food, or something else.

I tasted very little but it hit me like a freight train, jolted my system, and I thought I might be sick. I wanted to fly out the window but could not manage to get off the table. I waited until I could manage my wings properly, then I experienced a new sensation.

I suddenly wanted to fertilize every female fly in Mexico. I remembered a conversation between Barbara and Adam where they spoke of the sexual effects of cocaine. This had to be the reason cocaine was so popular. Adam, to Barbara's horror, had wanted her to not only try it, but loan him money so he could acquire it and resell the white powder at a substantial profit. She would have none of it.

That same evening, I flew a little closer to El Brazo to observe him in greater detail. He did not drink like his followers. Instead, he was channel surfing on the giant television set in his bedroom. He searched through a pile of pirated films and videos that had been obtained for his entertainment and found the movie entitled "Hope" starring Barbara (Esperanza in Spanish), which was also the character's name of the woman played by Barbara.

The movie was a worldwide hit by now, and El Brazo was eager to see it. He watched it from beginning to end without moving from his leather couch. Then he replayed it, stopping the film at the big love scene with Barbara and her leading man. It was tastefully done but revealed too much of her luscious body for my taste.

I was deflated by seeing Barbara so overtly displayed for public viewing. I had seen far more of her living together as we did in Malibu, but that was different.

I was no stranger to her, unlike all the men viewing her in this movie. I would not be comparing her to my wife or girlfriend, mentally and emotionally cheating on them. These same men would use her image to arouse themselves. I could not see this form of approval as adulation or appreciation. Thank heaven that flies are not so inclined.

Chapter 24
Amor

When the movie was over El Brazo was no longer interested in the Mexican peasant girls who vied for his attention. He talked about the movie and Barbara with his lieutenants.

Then he went back to the giant screen and replayed the movie twice more for them. When he was finally done with the movie he was energized and departed with his top guys to the library where he ignored the still-open maps and charts. My language skills were limited, but I kept hearing Malibu, Los Angeles, over and over, along with the word "sequester."

The next day, I encountered Juan making his weekly food delivery. He had stopped outside the kitchen to speak with one of El Brazo's top lieutenants, a shaven-headed, tall, thin man who spoke English and Spanish to Juan. He had the look of a really bad dude, maybe part American and part Mexican.

Dude: "Amigo, yo quiero una caja de ciggaros en Apatzingán. ¿Es possible?"

Juan: "Si, compadre. ¿Como esta?"

Dude: "Muy bueno. Might be making a trip to California."

Juan: "¿Porque?"

Dude: "Para sequester la chica rubia."

Juan: "¿Quien es la chica rubia?

Dude: "Esperanza, Hope, la actriz famosa. El Brazo esta enamorado con la chica rubia."

Juan: "He wants to kidnap her. But why?"

Dude: "Because he knows how to do it and he is the best ever."

I heard the name Hope, the famous actress. I got actress and El Brazo enamored. As soon as I heard the word "kidnap", I knew I had to get word to Johnny Ray.

My involvement with drug smuggling was now secondary to my need to protect Barbara from El Brazo. I had memorized enough information that Johnny Ray could use the same way I conveyed information to Barbara and that would have to satisfy him.

Los Proscritos had people in New York, Los Angeles, South America, Asia, and everywhere. And they had plenty of experience when it came to kidnapping. El Brazo had personally trained his minions, and successfully negotiated with state and federal officials, frightened billionaires, and law enforcement czars for enormous sums of money. Sometimes the money procured the safe returns of the victims. Sometimes it did not. If anyone knew the ins and outs of a kidnapping plot and its execution, it would be El Brazo. Perhaps he was bored with drugs and small-time operations that generated fear in opposing cartels, but lacked dramatic impact.

He was young and ambitious and could be thinking of the world stage. An operation so daring and dangerous that it would become an instant legend, to say nothing of being an international event of the greatest magnitude.

He could use it to embarrass the Mexican government; display the ineptness of the Federales; and demonstrate the superiority of Los Proscritos over the other cartels, in Mexico and beyond. The mountain boys from Michoacán would be world news.

Songs would be written and sung forever, movies would be spawned and poetry would flourish in the minds and hearts of his people. And, of course, there was Barbara. El Brazo thought, she probably had never known a real man, just those Hollywood maricones. He would show her what it was like to be with a real man. El Brazo was that man.

My last and best guess is that El Brazo was love-struck, a wholly peculiar human folly. I had observed this trait directly. Barbara herself was a good example. Her ex-boyfriend, Jeff, lied to her from the moment they met. He lied about his education, he lied about his business experience, he lied about the car accident when he injured another human, and he lied about his motivation for selling Barbara a Beverly Hills mansion.

His lame explanations were ignored by Barbara because she was in love with him. If the same lies had been told to her by any other person, she would have rejected that person instantly.

Barbara and I had watched endless movies and television in which love was the motivation for the show. A man or woman acted beyond the accepted boundaries of society, or out of character and the explanation was often their love for another human. A beautiful woman with the benefit of excellent education, wealth, and family support falls in love with a homely, dangerous maniac just out of prison for some heinous crime. It makes no sense, but love is the explanation when no other is logically available.

If one of the characters has to suffer, it's for love. If the character loses his or her bearings and acts crazy, it's because of love. Heroic, often impossible acts are driven by love, no matter if the object of love is unworthy, disinterested, or dismissive. Once the love idea is planted in the human brain, reason, intelligence, experience, and good judgment depart instantly in favor of this ambiguous, treacherous concept.

Even dangerous gang leaders can experience love because they are still human. However, their love has to be expressed differently from their followers; more grandiose, more powerful, more undefinable. In literature, they call it the "grand passion."

If most leaders fail to have this event in the course of their lives, then surely they have been cheated of the ultimate life experience.

It is unthinkable that a great leader of men would be denied a "grand passion" as he has defined himself as that possessor of unique qualities and therefore a worthy candidate. There would be no cheating El Brazo of his intent to possess the unattainable. Love, desire, passion, obsession, call it what you will. It is unsettling, even dangerous; like a force of nature.

The hurricane that levels vast sections of towns, ships, homes, vehicles, trees, and plants doesn't apologize for itself. It just is what it is. The same is true of an earthquake that shatters glass, wood, and steel to fall upon the helpless women and children trapped beneath the debris by no fault of their own.

The mindless, unstoppable force of nature, that impulse called love is not so different from the hurricanes, the earthquakes, and the violent seas. It resides in the human brain and breast, ready to strike, unpredictable and uncontained.

Pity the unsuspecting object of the "grand passion."

Chapter 25
The Bust

How does an insignificant fly fight off a blood-thirsty narco-terrorist Mexican gang, hell-bent on kidnapping a defenseless Hollywood movie star? How does a mute fly tell the FBI the details of a kidnapping plan? I might as well forget about sleeping because these questions lit up my thoughts night and day. Worse, I had to decide whether I should follow the plan to reconnect with the "mole" and go back to the FBI with the details of the drug smuggling operation or stick with El Brazo to learn the details of the kidnap plan.

He would soon be leaving the compound near Apatzingán. I heard different destinations floated, as El Brazo often changed plans at the last moment for reasons of security. He might be going to Zatacuaro, or possibly Morelia, or Lazaro Cardenas, or none of the above.

Another consideration affected by my choice would be Juan. If the mole did not have me in the glass container when we met with Johnny Ray in Morelia, there would be hell to pay. The mole would have to make up his own story. He could tell his masters that I was swatted and crushed like any ordinary fly.

Johnny Ray would carry on about the loss of a device that cost more than an aircraft carrier, but that would be for the benefit of the mole. Johnny Ray would be pissed about losing the opportunity to take credit for a huge drug bust, but my demise would not trouble him, or the FBI for long. I doubted that the FBI even knew about me.

After hearing the word kidnap from the mouth of El Brazo's top lieutenant, I jumped into Juan's pickup truck and hid under the passenger seat waiting for him to return. As soon as he cleared the road to the Hacienda, I began buzzing, jumping from place to place, and acting as crazy as I could. This went on at length until Juan placed a call to Johnny Ray for instructions.

Juan: "Senor, the device is loco. It won't stop flying around in circles, it flies around my face, and it buzzes like it's going to blow up. What do I do?"

Johnny Ray: "Treat it just like it's a fly. Give it some water and fruit. It won't explode or damage you. It has been programmed to do this. Meet me at the warehouse in Morelia as fast as you can. I'll be there."

Juan: "What if the fly won't get in the bottle, or he blows up or flies out the window and goes away? What do I do?"

Johnny Ray: "Show him the bottle. This is part of the program. He will get into the bottle. It's in the program, but first, give him water and food."

I did exactly as Johnny Ray directed, and Juan calmed down as we chugged onward to

Morelia. Johnny Ray was waiting for us. He gave the mole a wad of bills, grabbed the glass container, and we headed for a hotel room in town.

He spread out detailed maps of the US and Mexico and I went to work trying to communicate what I knew. I landed on the beach location, buzzed, hopped up and down, then went to Morelia, then to San Antonio, the US distribution point. It was like playing charades, with lots of bad guesses by the agent, much redundancy, and acting by me. We played the buzz game: One buzz for no, two buzzes for yes, and three for I don't know.

Johnny Ray: "They are bringing in drugs from the coast."

Two buzzes.

Johnny Ray: "It's cocaine, right!"

Yes.

Johnny Ray: "Lots of cocaine."

Yes.

Johnny Ray: "It's being trucked to Morelia. Then it goes to San Antonio."

Yes, again.

Johnny Ray: "Where does it go in Morelia?"

I don't know.

Johnny Ray: "Shit."

Johnny Ray: "Where does it go in San Antonio?"

No answer.

Johnny Ray: "Goddamn it, answer me! Do you know where it goes?"

Yes.

He started guessing, but he never got to the word bakery. There was a menu for room service and I flew onto it and hopped up and down.

Johnny Ray opened the menu and read from it. I became active and agitated when he reached the section with tortillas and tacos.

Johnny Ray: "Tortillas, and tacos. The coke is stashed in the tortillas or is it the tacos?"

Yes.

Johnny Ray: "Which one? One buzz for tortillas, two buzzes for tacos."

Two buzzes.

Johnny Ray: "Who gets the tacos?"

It took him more than a few tries but he finally got around to bakeries. I had been all over the menu on breads and baked goods.

Johnny Ray: "Yeah, I got it. Bakeries, they always work at night so trucks and people moving around at night are normal for bakeries."

He immediately got on the satellite phone to start a search for every Mexican bakery in San Antonio.

Johnny Ray: "So, when does this all happen?"

I don't know.

Johnny Ray: "Is it soon?"

Yes.

He was confused when I also landed on the map showing the port at Lazaro Cardenas. We established that it wasn't more cocaine, that it was at the same time, and that it wasn't marijuana or any other drug. He finally got the idea that it was nothing but a diversion.

Now came the hard part, the kidnapping. Johnny Ray was ready to call it a night. He was tired of mentally flailing about with a mute insect. I wouldn't let him go, and buzzed madly around his head until he came back to the makeshift desk with the maps piled on it.

Johnny Ray: "Okay, there's something else, is that it?"

Two buzzes, yes.

Johnny Ray: "Does it involve the same drug cartel?"

Same response.

Johnny Ray: "They want to murder someone?"

No.

Johnny Ray: "They want something from someone?"

Yes.

Johnny Ray: "They want money, guns, gold, tanks, airplanes, land. What else do drug cartels do? They kidnap people and torture them, is that it?"

YES, YES, YES.

Johnny Ray: "So, who do they want to kidnap, Michelle Obama?"

No.

Johnny Ray: "Who is it? Someone you know?"

Yes, again.

Johnny Ray: "Well, you only know two people in this world besides me. Barbara and Mrs. Olson. That makes it too easy, because we would beg them to take Mrs. Olson. It has to be Barbara."

Yes.

Johnny Ray: "Its Los Proscritos vs. the FBI. A slam dunk."

Maybe not, I thought to myself, having experienced the FBI in action.

Chapter 26
The Hero Returns

Johnny Ray and I returned to LA and took up residence in his Pasadena condo. It wasn't much to look at, but it beat imprisonment by Mrs. Olson. There were a few changes, mainly more photos of Johnny Ray from the shows and movie parts Barbara's agent had secured for him. When he wasn't pestering the talent agent, Johnny Ray was on the phone non-stop to the mole in Mexico for information about where and what El Brazo was doing.

The FBI was lining up its resources to make the big drug bust in San Antonio, with its agents and their Mexican counterparts following the trail as the cocaine came ashore on the Sinaloa coast.

We had been back a week when the big shipment arrived. The whole FBI operation went off like clockwork; Los Proscritos was monitored at every juncture with the big payoff coming in San Antonio, the seizure of multimillions of dollars of cocaine, and the arrest of many innocents.

Los Proscritos' caravan of drivers were innocent victims. The people in the bakery had no knowledge of the cocaine baggies that had been inserted into the food at the meth labs along the roads from Apatzingan to Morelia, then to San Antonio. Nevertheless, they were rounded up to face Mexican justice and displayed in the press to demonstrate the enormous reach of the gang.

Johnny Ray got big-time points from the FBI. Medals, promotions, bonus payments, and bragging rights. Juan told him that El Brazo was pissed beyond belief. The mole thought it was a good time to leave Michoacán and the FBI pulled him out without much argument.

Unfortunately, that removed our only source of information and left us guessing as to how the kidnap operation would proceed. Still, you can't blame the mole for leaving. No point in becoming a corpse message if you have a choice in the matter.

Johnny Ray was nice enough to bring me along when he had his periodic meetings with Barbara. Our reunion took place in Barbara's Malibu house, the scene of the FBI near shoot-out over my capture. Barbara was all smiles, even a little misty-eyed. Johnny Ray grudgingly told her about my role in the Mexican drug busts, reserving the true hero's role for himself as the mastermind of the entire operation.

The mole, who lived in daily fear of decapitation, was acknowledged as a helpful tool. I had followed Johnny Ray's instructions in my supporting role, thereby earning the right to continue with the FBI under his supervision, probably without authorization from the higher-ups. I did not savor continuing my time as a spy.

I was so happy to be back in Malibu and close to Barbara that I paid little or no attention to the official FBI version, as delivered by Johnny Ray. I landed on Barbara's soft bare shoulder and she acknowledged me without a brush off. Our tactile connection, harmless and superficial, meant everything to me. I felt encouraged, rewarded, justified, and proud. She walked and talked with Johnny Ray and I rode with her, never moving from her warmth, drinking in her essence, barely listening until Johnny Ray came to the subject of our visit, the kidnap plot.

Johnny Ray: (blurting) "I don't want to scare you, but we think this Mexican drug lord wants to kidnap you."

Barbara: "You can't be serious."

Johnny Ray: "We think he means it. He's bored with drugs, money, guns, and murder. He got his start with kidnapping government officials and their families for ransom, so he knows how to do it."

Barbara: "Why me, I'm just a Hollywood actress, not a political opponent."

Johnny Ray: "You're a world-famous movie star, and if he took you it would make him world-famous."

Barbara: "Surely our government would get involved and he's no match for our military."

Johnny Ray: "Well, the Mexican government is an ally, and we can't very well invade an ally to save you. There would be intense diplomatic pressure applied, but El Brazo could care less about that. Their government's military has proven itself incapable of dealing with the drug cartels, especially on their home turf. It's a classic Mexican stand-off with you in the middle."

Barbara: (in a demanding tone) "Where does this kidnap information come from."

He pointed at me perched on Barbara's shoulder.

Johnny Ray: "Comes from your boy there."

We then reverted to our old question-and-answer buzzing method and I confirmed what Johnny Ray had told her. It was so remote and seemed so impossible that Barbara did not appear openly frightened by the bizarre possibility that she could be the kidnap victim of a rural Mexican drug boss.

Barbara: "So what should I do about this?"

Johnny Ray had to admit that he didn't have a clue, just wanted to let her know that something was in the wind. He talked about putting me back in action if the kidnappers were spotted anywhere outside of their usual places.

He actually floated the idea of using Barbara as bait to capture El Brazo. No chance that I would play along with that program. She wasn't thrilled with the idea of the FBI pimping her to El Brazo as bait.

Barbara: "This whole thing is ridiculous."

Johnny Ray: "Mexico is ridiculous. In case you haven't noticed it's total chaos down there. The gangs run the country now and if they were politically motivated, they could take it over. They have more arms, more money, and more popular support than any police force. The army can't control the gangs because they have more and better weapons and fighters who are better trained than the army goons, most of whom are on the take and hated by the people. If they kidnapped you I don't how we would ever get you back. They would demand billions of dollars, so who pays that?"

Barbara looked thoughtful and offered the first meaningful comment on the potential kidnap caper.

Barbara: "I need security, and not FBI, and not retired cops."

Johnny Ray: "So who is that?"

Barbara: "You wait and see. I have an idea. I need to do some research."

Chapter 27
Women to the Rescue

Barbara's idea was to surround herself with women adept in self-defense, and firearms, and fluent in Spanish. They would be her first line of defense. At least the Los Proscritos gang members would not shoot them or behead them. It was a policy strictly prohibited and enforced within the organization.

Women would be better companions. More empathetic and more intuitive to Barbara's needs, moods, and fears. They would feel more like concerned friends than intruders and she could learn from them. Communication would be more open, and less affected by the inevitable complications that accompany any male/female interaction.

In a short time, she gathered two women to act as her bodyguards and installed them in her house. One was an Asian martial artist, the other was a Mexican bodybuilder. They worked out daily, either on the beach or at a local gym, and soon Barbara was looking more fit, toned, and healthy. She gave up her bridge games for martial arts training, weights, Spanish lessons, and Japanese lessons.

The bodyguards went everywhere with Barbara. They took all their meals together, went to work with Barbara when she was on a shoot, and stood with and by her for interviews and photo shoots. Johnny Ray was skeptical of their ability.

The one secret Barbara would not share with her bodyguards was me. I could not hang around in Malibu as I would be noticed, and most likely to be dealt with in summary fashion if I was discovered. I continued to live with Johnny Ray, who was now somewhat of a hero in the local law enforcement world. He visited Barbara or met her in town for lunch at secure locations to discuss her safety and security. I went along on these visits.

Barbara was a magnet for fans, autograph hunters, and paparazzi. When someone became too aggressive, the bodyguards closed in. They were polite with fans, but firm. They were a bit firmer with the photographers and pushy autograph hunters. There were times when they handled people physically, but never with extreme force or aggression. They were careful to do the minimum, but in such a way that the fan, the photographer, the drunk and the just plain nosy were aware that much more would follow if they resisted.

Natividad, the Hispanic woman, was a health food and vitamin freak, but a terrific cook. She took over the kitchen, the shopping, and the meal schedule. She was relentless about her workouts and diet. The Asian girl, Hilo, was quieter and more reserved. She had her daily routine of meditation, reading, and a martial arts workout.

She was very slim, yet ate like a horse. No matter what Nati put in front of her, she ate every last bite. A plate cleaner like Hilo could have put me out of business if I lived there.

Johnny Ray remained critical of Barbara's security. He put up with it for a few months until he couldn't hold it back. He now talked to me as a confidant about Barbara's safety.

Johnny Ray: "I can't force her to fire them. She needs something, but we can't spare the people for security when all we have is a rumor that there could be a kidnap attempt. I could never tell anyone where the rumor began or who brought it to me. These girls are Charlie's Angel wannabes. I'm going to demonstrate this to you."

The result of the conversation was that Johnny Ray would test the ability of the girls to foil a kidnap. He was certain that it would expose them and undermine Barbara's faith in her Amazon women.

Late on a Friday night, while Barbara and Nati were engrossed in a re-run of "Lost" the front door was suddenly thrown open to reveal a single figure holding a pistol, dressed in black with a nylon mask pulled over his face. He pointed a pistol at the rear wall that separated the living room from the kitchen.

Intruder: (in a muffled voice) "Everyone up against the wall."

Time slowed down as Barbara and Nati slowly stood to move from the couch toward the wall. When they stood facing the wall, he told them to kneel with their faces pressed against the wall. The masked intruder approached them and prodded his gun into Barbara's neck and told her to get to her feet and back up slowly, while maintaining the pressure of the gun against her neck.

Nati spoke rapidly to the man in Spanish, telling him he would never get away with a kidnap, the FBI was everywhere around the house.

The gunman paid no attention. Barbara commenced screaming. His answer was to click off the safety on his pistol as he moved and held the gun against Barbara's ear.

Intruder: (growling in Barbara's ear) "Silence."

He squeezed her neck and backed toward the door with Barbara in tow. Before he reached the door, Hilo came screaming from the hallway that connected the living room to the bedrooms. She had been meditating in her room and heard the commotion in the living room. She flew at the intruder, executing a picture-perfect scissor kick to the head of the man holding Barbara.

Nati leaped off the floor and made for the kidnapper with the first weapon in sight, a picture frame she grabbed off a table next to the couch.

By the time Nati crossed the room to do battle, Hilo was on the ground and the intruder had dumped Barbara on top of her. He subdued Nati instantly, picture frame and all, with a swift move that caught her off guard, and she joined the pile on the floor.

He then ripped off his mask, tossed the unloaded gun onto the couch, and helped the women to their feet. Hilo and Nati wanted to continue the fight, but it was useless. Barbara was in total shock and clung to Nati, her head buried in her shoulder, unable to look at Johnny Ray.

Johnny Ray: "I apologize folks, but we had to do this. I could have hurt or shot Nati and Hilo, and jumped into a waiting car in seconds with Barbara. My accomplices would have stuffed a rag in her mouth, bound her hands and feet, and she would be mine. We have to assume the kidnappers are experienced, probably trained in Krav Maga, a little bit of which I just used against Nati and Hilo. Next stop, an abandoned airstrip in Oxnard and a private plane takes her god knows where."

Nati: (bleating) "You surprised us, it wasn't a fair test."

Johnny Ray: "Of course it was. Kidnappers don't wait for invitations."

Hilo: "You knew the layout of the house, and you knew how many of us there were."

Johnny Ray: "Believe me, they will know the same things."

Barbara: (relieved) "Where did you get that stupid mask?"

Johnny Ray: (grinning) "My last movie role. I played a rogue cop."

Barbara: "No doubt, a dramatic portrayal for the ages."

If he wasn't careful, Barbara would drag him to an acting class to polish up his technique. He had video of all his performances and I had watched them with growing horror. My advice would have been that time-honored bromide; don't give up your day job.

Chapter 28
The Swarm

Kidnap-wise we were back to square one. After failing the test, Nati and Hilo resolved to be more diligent. They redoubled their efforts to be on high alert without any let-up. Barbara recognized their downside, but she was just too attached to them to terminate their employment.

Since my return from foreign duty, very little, if anything had been heard about El Brazo. After many months of no activity, speculation had it that he might have been murdered by a rival gang, or by one of his own people in Los Proscritos. For whatever reason, El Brazo had gone missing.

It came down to me. I had to figure out a way to stop him, to slow him down, and then derail his love train. I couldn't rely on the FBI to devote time and resources to something so improbable as a Mexican drug lord snatching a world-famous actress in a brazen kidnap. Local police were not even in the equation.

Well-meaning girls like Nati and Hilo were no match for heavily armed religious fanatics. I was slow to reach the inevitable conclusion that humans could not, or would not, protect their own. I would have to rely on the only source available to me: the world of flies.

An old movie gave me an idea. I had seen it on late-night television, where all old, bad movies sometimes find a second life. It was called "The Swarm," and by all accounts, it is one of the worst movies ever made. Killer bees come from Africa to America and in such huge numbers that they threaten to disrupt the entirety of human society. There it was, fear and hatred of insects, the human species Achilles heel. I would find a way to make it work against El Brazo.

First, I had to reconnect with the world of flies. It was time to face this issue because I had been avoiding it my whole life. The insect creed is to lay down your life for the good of the species. No questions asked.

Ants are always given as the prime example, and next to ants, flies look like freelance thrill-seekers. But that's wrong because it just happens that ants are at the very top when it comes to insect discipline. Flies understand what it means to work together, to sacrifice for the greater good of the group; while not eating, that is. It's the gift of flight that gives the illusion of total freedom to the fly, not any inherent desire to go it alone.

I decided to reconnect by going back to my roots. I hung out at Gelson's in Calabasas, staying nights and days away from Malibu and Pasadena. I managed to convince Barbara and Johnny Ray that I needed to be on my own, with my own kind.

It wasn't easy to alter my eating habits, but I forced myself to consume what my fellows lived on. I networked among the groups and individuals and built some trust among both leaders and followers. I did what all flies do. I fertilized eggs, located and shared the best garbage with my group, slept in makeshift shelters, and taught the young ones what to avoid.

Having lived so long my advice came to be accepted. I was not ridiculed for my age. Instead, I found respect. Perhaps my physical appearance counted for something, but that wore off quickly enough. I emphasized the importance of working together as a group, and encouraged the local population to be wary of people, but not frightened.

I told them of my experiences, of riding in cars and airplanes, about the White House, New York, Las Vegas, and Mexico. Some chose to laugh at my stories and disbelieve my adventures, but many found a window to a wider world through me. I told them about Barbara after I first explained what a movie star was.

I told them about Johnny Ray and explained what the FBI was. I told them about El Brazo, and what we had to do to protect Barbara from him. A sense of purpose grew among us. We were no longer merely victims or outcasts. We had a mission and a means.

We began with some training exercises involving the unsuspecting patrons of Gelson's market. We would select a target and employ the swarm technique.

I would lead by flying into the path of the person emerging from the market on the way to their car.

Thirty or forty flies would come right behind me and envelope the unsuspecting shopper. The flies would buzz and stay close without landing on the person, forming a sort of barrier. The idea was not to just frighten the person being swarmed, it was to test his or her reaction as well as the responses of other persons in the parking lot.

In most cases, the person got a little panicky when swarmed. The reaction of other people was to avoid the swarm, rather than extend help. They wanted no part of the person with the flies about them, perhaps believing that there was a reason for the flies to be attracted to them, like an unpleasant odor or a noxious substance being carried by the host. We experimented with the number of flies needed to create the desired effect, sometimes with as many as a hundred flies at a time enveloping a shopper, other times as few as ten. There was always some reaction.

Knowing that we could be taken seriously by humans was a major step. Now it remained to determine how our abilities could best be used in a positive way.

Complaints were made to the market, but were brushed aside by management as coincidence or exaggeration. When they noticed fewer cars in the parking lot and a decline in business, they responded by spraying the parking lot with chemicals that could only harm humans. No further action was taken to deal with "the fly problem." However, we needed one more test case and it presented itself shortly after management sprayed the parking lot.

Toward the end of the day, I came across a young woman, in her late teens, carrying a load of groceries to her parked car at the very furthest part of the lot from the store entrance. A young man, in his late teens, sloppily dressed, was nonchalantly following the woman from a distance.

She had opened the car and was placing her groceries in the rear seat behind the driver's seat when the would-be assailant arrived behind her and tried to embrace her. She resisted and struck at him, but he caught her hand and then ripped the front of the woman's blouse, buttons popping in and around her grocery bag.

I lost no time in summoning the army of flies, which must have reached at least one hundred, and led them to the car, where the man was trying to push the woman into the back seat of the car. He had pulled her shirt off and stuffed it into her mouth. She was on her back squirming and fighting her attacker while he remained half-bent over outside the car fighting his way in with his pants lowered below his hips. I ordered the flies to surround him and buzz menacingly as they flew in circles about him.

The teenager was immediately distracted, as was the tearful woman. She cried, he yanked up his pants and made a run for it away from the car right into the arms of the market's security guard. Our swarm broke off and we disappeared into the night. We had our proof that the swarm effectively prevented a rape, no violence was needed to do so and the young woman had been saved from a negative, life-changing event. I knew then that we were ready for even more serious work. I knew I could lead troops and that my army was loyal to me, brave, and unafraid of human confrontation.

The very next morning Barbara came looking for me. She told me that the story of the incident in the parking lot had made the morning papers.

Barbara: "It says here that a swarm of flies had prevented the rape of a nineteen-year-old girl in Gelson's parking lot. The assailant was an eighteen-year-old boy who was frightened by a whirling, buzzing mass of scary insects and attempted to flee the scene when he was apprehended by a security guard who acknowledged the role of the flies in the rescue. The guard said he was proud of the flies. He was interviewed on Channel five shortly afterward and said, "Those flies have more guts than the patrons of the market. "

Barbara: "You had a hand in this didn't you?"

I buzzed twice.

Barbara: "I've missed you Fly. I want you to come with me to look at a house in Beverly Hills tomorrow. About two months ago, Jeff leased out this mansion to an Argentine film producer for $50,000 a month. When the lease is up the house will be for sale and he wants me to buy it. It's a steal he said. A once-in-a-lifetime opportunity. He says this producer wants to meet me for a film he's doing in Argentina, with locations in Brazil, Argentina, and Beverly Hills.

Barbara: (continuing) "I don't trust Jeff and I don't see much of him, but he wants to do something that will make up for some of his mistakes, and his lies, so I agreed to let him show me this property and meet this producer named Hector Locarno. I want you to come with me. Jeff will know you are there, although we never talked about you. He had his suspicions, but your presence will keep him in check."

We met Jeff at a place near the Beverly Hills Hotel, just south of Sunset. He was extolling the virtues of the location and the history of the home, which had once belonged to a studio head.

A butler in full dress answered the door and showed us into the foyer. He looked familiar to me, but I just couldn't place him.

We waited in the foyer at the foot of a winding staircase for the current tenant to make his appearance. After a short delay, he emerged dramatically, tango music playing in the background. Jeff did the introductions. It reminded me of a movie I saw with Barbara. I just can't remember the name. Hector came to meet us, dancing down the stairs, a gay and colorful gaucho, determined to make the theatrical entrance that defined his movie character. He must have seen the same movie that Barbara and I watched in Malibu.

Jeff: "Hector Locarno, meet Barbara Gardner."

Hector: (in slightly accented English) "May I call you Barbara? Delighted to meet you at last."

Barbara: (mumbling) "Likewise."

Hector had mixed a pitcher of Argentina's favorite cocktail and insisted on pouring drinks for Jeff and Barbara.

Hector: "You must see this house that your wonderful Jeff found for me."

He led Jeff and Barbara on the tour, dropping names and anecdotes about the history of the house. The party where Judy Garland fell in the pool, the time that Gene Kelley danced on the marble table, the night Dean Martin passed out in the bathroom, and the starlet who was with him. Somebody had done some detailed, but meaningless Hollywood research.

Hector had set out to charm Barbara and was working hard at it. He had brought with him a collection of Argentine paintings and sculptures which he proudly displayed in the massive formal living room. There were Argentine rugs in the den and matching tapestries, the themes of which he explained to Barbara.

The more of Hector I saw, the more he seemed familiar. I didn't catch it at first, but then it clicked. El Brazo, without the mustache, a designer haircut, twenty-five pounds lighter, dressed in an Armani shirt and slacks, with hand-worked Italian leather shoes.

He had worked hard on his English and his new identity, but still had the arms and chest of a weightlifter, only minus the tattoos. He had been to see a plastic surgeon somewhere to remove the tattoos and smooth out the acne scars on his face. However, he still had that presence about him, a person accustomed to command, accustomed to being praised, obeyed, and listened to. He had the indefinable quality of weight, something that a person like Jeff lacked entirely.

The difference was that Jeff chattered while Hector spoke sparingly, but with substance. I wasn't sure if Barbara made this distinction, but she did seem intrigued by Hector. She did not object when Jeff and Hector made dinner plans for the following night at the Beverly Hills Hotel after drinks in the Polo Lounge.

Hector: "Three for dinner at seven?"

Barbara: "Let's say five, if you don't mind. I'd like my girlfriends to come along. You'll love them."

Hector: "Beautiful, I can't wait."

Chapter 29
The Kidnap Foiled

El Brazo, Hector, had a plan, but it didn't seem to be a brute force kidnapping. More like a seduction. He had gone to great lengths to remake himself to fit the plan. He had done his research and found Jeff, who paved the way for Barbara. He probably knew much more, but he didn't know about me.

My first move was to assemble my team when Barbara dropped me off at Gelson's that evening. I gathered at least 500 flies for a rally. This would be my first oration to the troops. They must be convinced that I could lead them to victory. They had to share with me the historical notion of a change in the interaction between insects and humans.

"This is the moment we have been waiting and training for. This is our moment to change history and show the world we are Dipterans, an order of insects to be reckoned with. We are not merely pests, spreaders of disease, objects of derision. We will not be victims any longer. We will unite to prevent an international incident that could take innocent lives."

"There may be collateral damage, but there will be no kidnapping, trust me, as long we follow the plan. There will be no media circus, but people will eventually know what we have accomplished. And, we will do it without violence."

"Yes, there could be danger to all of us. Our non-violent behavior could provoke violence from more than one source. We could be rejected, ridiculed, and our very existence questioned. Be strong, each and every one of you. Be ready to follow me and follow your dreams to a new world of respect. Our first stage will be departure this very evening."

I laid it on pretty thick. It was really my dream, not theirs. There would be some collateral damage and flies could perish, but most of them would be dead within thirty days anyway. I could not see the harm in inspiring them to step out of the shadows. I was mildly ashamed that I found this demagogue business to be so enjoyable.

All 500 responded with a buzz that could be heard in Van Nuys. We would move out in the darkness tonight, flying in loose formation to Sportsmen's Lodge on Ventura Boulevard where it intersects with Coldwater Canyon. We would refresh, feed, and regroup.

I promised every last fly that soon we would dine in Beverly Hills among movie stars, captains of industry, and the beautiful people. Truffles and champagne to celebrate. Our final destination was the Beverly Hills Hotel, but first, we must bivouac at Sportsmen's Lodge on Coldwater Canyon, to be refreshed and ready for tomorrow.

The flies could not have been happier. I confirmed the truism that an army marches on its belly, something every leader should remember. We found an outbuilding on the property in which to gather and spend the night after gorging on the house specialty, fresh trout. Flying miles had exhausted the troops and a full-blown fish feast had them full and refreshed. They would be ready for the remaining flight and the implementation of our strategy to protect Barbara.

Early the next morning our determined force rose to cross the mountains to test themselves and meet their fate. We lost a few members to several ravens at the Getty Museum. They descended on us before we could escape underneath some parked cars. It was a reminder that predators are everywhere. First, we will deal with the humans. The others, if encountered, come later.

We reached the Beverly Hills Hotel in the afternoon. I stationed groups at strategic entries and exits, to be called into play if needed. Then our lead group flew across Sunset Boulevard into Hector's rented grounds and mansion. This time there were faces I recognized from my stay in Michoacán. The gardeners, the drivers, the valet, and the cooks were all Los Proscritos. No doubt they were armed to the teeth. They might intimidate other people but flies are another matter. Nobody has ever shot a fly with an AK-47 or an AR-15, at least not to my knowledge.

With ten other flies, we infiltrated the house and found El Brazo getting ready for the early evening dinner. We buzzed around, gradually establishing our presence, and he paid no attention to us. He proceeded to shower, brush his teeth, and select from his closet the proper clothes, expensive, not too flashy or overdressed. He did not want to stand out at dinner but he was careful to add the right accoutrements. A large diamond Rolex President, a fresh set of Italian loafers, and an Argentine national flag pin on his jacket.

When El Brazo, that is Hector, left the bedroom to go downstairs, we all stayed with him. He went to the kitchen for a snack and he found nothing unusual about flies in the kitchen. Our first five flies moved in a little closer, moving around his legs quietly so as not to gain too much attention.

Over the next hour, the rest of our cadre moved into the action, getting more coverage. From time to time El Brazo brushed away the flies, who each time backed off and then slowly returned to be near the man, without pressing in close.

The brush-offs became more frequent until we backed away, buzzed the room, and slowly returned to our formation. El Brazo was becoming annoyed about the time the front doorbell rang, announcing Jeff, Barbara, Nati, and Hilo. Our strategy was playing out as planned.

The usual greetings, formalities, embraces, and air kisses followed the introductions. Next came drinks, the house tour, the history of fascinating objects within the house, and other trivia leading up to dinner. Nati spoke Spanish to Hector, who replied comfortably in his native tongue.

Hector spoke of his desire to bring Hollywood productions to his native Argentina, and I began to sense the details of his kidnap/seduction plan for Barbara. He would lure her to Argentina on the pretext of making a film, pursue her romantically, and if that failed, he would kidnap her to Mexico where he was invulnerable. He was certain he would not fail in the romance department.

Hector was so absorbed in the conversation that he didn't notice the increasing presence of the flies. However, Barbara was on it right away and recognized that I was up to something but she wasn't sure what it was. She decided to say nothing and wait. Nati, on the other hand, plunged right into the subject by telling Hector in Spanish that he had too many flies in his house. His solution was to suggest they get out of the house and onto the Polo Lounge.

The party decamped from the house and went in one of Hector's enormous SUVs across the street to the hotel. My full group of flies arrived at about the same time as Hector prepared to enter the Polo Lounge, which was filled with the usual agents, producers, wannabes, and hangers-on.

As we waited for the attention of the maître d' to lead the group to a booth in the Polo Lounge, we initiated a partial swarm. At least fifty flies surrounded Hector.

At first, he tried to brush the flies away. Then Nati and Hilo gave a half-hearted try at dispersing the cloud of flies. Hector excused himself to the men's room with flies attached. He looked in the mirror, urinated, brushed off his clothing from head to toe, swatted at his person, and looked inside his jacket and pants to see if there was anything there to attract flies. His face was flushed beneath his tan, and the heat and sweat were pouring off him.

Frustrated, he returned to the group standing with the maître d', still surrounded by a cadre of flies. By now other patrons were noticing this odd person and his insect armada.

Maître d': "Sir, I don't believe we can seat your party in the lounge or the main room."

Hector slipped him five hundred dollars. The maître d' gestured towards the men's room.

Maître d': "Perhaps you would like the assistance of our staff? This way, please."

Several waiters gathered around Hector, striking at the flies with towels, spraying vapors of insect repellent, and dousing him with water. I ordered my minions to back off. Hector composed himself and returned sheepishly to the waiting group, which was seated in a booth next to an outdoor exit. Leading the attack, we went at Hector again with renewed vigor as soon as Hector and the others were seated.

Within moments everyone in the room was staring at the table, and Hector in particular. Some approached to get a better look at this peculiar sight. Conversation in the room dwindled to a hushed murmur at the spectacle of a man enveloped by flies.

Hector was beside himself with embarrassment and rage. The rest of the table was focused on him, unable to look away, unable to make the usual small talk and banter. Any romantic notion that Hector sought to promote with Barbara was stone-cold dead. Hector was cursing in Spanish under his breath. Nati appeared to be shocked by what she was hearing.

Hector looked for and found the nearest exit out of the Polo Lounge. He did not give or need an explanation. As he made his way onto the patio outside the main room, another wave of flies came at him, so dense that he could barely be seen from the table.

Now he was flailing at the flies, cursing in Spanish, swatting at us, striking nothing. He jumped, twisted, and pulled at his clothing.

Hector: (screaming in English) "Help me, help me."

His help came from an unexpected source. Barbara leaped to her feet and rushed outside to join Hector.

Barbara: (shouting at the files) "Stop it, go away, stop torturing this man, leave him alone."

I backed away and called off the attack. Suddenly he was standing alone with Barbara, the flies gone behind a hedge. He was choking back tears of rage and fear.

Hector: "How did you do that?"

Barbara: "I have no idea, but I could not stand to see you suffer that way and I had to do something."

Hector: (softly) "Your kindness is beyond my ability to understand. Those people inside were enjoying my discomfort, and I was powerless to stop the flies. Only you could save me, and I will never know why. I will thank the Lord for sending you to deliver me from the plague of the flies."

She held out her hand and led him inside, back to the waiting party at their table. Hector, still visibly shaken, could only shake his head and offer apologies. He continued to cross himself, oblivious to everyone around him. He mumbled something about the plague several times in Spanish.

Barbara: "I think we should call it a night."

All agreed, and Hector promptly returned to his rental home. Only Barbara knew what really happened and she wasn't about to share that knowledge with anyone.

The next morning there was an article in the LA Times about the strange happenings at the Polo Lounge. A photograph of Hector, his body surrounded by flies, his face clear as a bell on the front page of the paper. The same photo appeared on the Yahoo home page. Someone had snapped a picture with a cell phone camera and posted it on Instagram, and from there it went viral.

By noon that same day, Hector and his gardeners, cooks, valets, and drivers had vacated the house and disappeared. There are some occupations where publicity just won't do.

I hadn't planned it this way, but it worked out even better than I anticipated. Later, I heard from Barbara that Nati had pegged Hector as Mexican, not Argentine. His cursing was uniquely Mexican by dialect and idiom.

His ramblings about the plague were confusing, but they referenced Los Proscritos and God's anger with him. Nati knew the setup was all a façade. To use her description, it was all photoshopped: The house, the furniture, the rugs, the art, the clothes. And Hector, who was never Hector.

Chapter 30
Are There Flies in Heaven?

The time after the Hector incident was hard for me. Should I go back to living with Barbara, go back to living with Johnny Ray and work for the FBI, or stay with my brave followers, the fearless flies? No matter what I did someone would feel hurt, and abandoned.

On the other hand, Barbara had Johnny Ray, the FBI, her fame, and female friends living with her. She could never disclose her relationship with me to them. The fans, the friends, and the as-yet-unknown men that would come into her life would never understand. She knew it. We had not chosen it, but we had to reluctantly disengage with one another.

The flies had each other. I was somewhere in between all of them. My life in L.A. seemed over and done with. I was too old to hang around race tracks scrounging for information. I had known presidents, drug lords, and movie stars to name just a few people of note. I had survived sneak attacks (the FBI), vicious killers, and bloodthirsty gangs. Was there anything left for me?

Without knowing it, I had aged considerably. I never saw it coming, although the leg and wing injuries I suffered in New York caused me more pain each day. Flight was no longer the pure delight it had been. Hearing, eyesight, strength, and stamina had all diminished without fair warning. No longer did the female flies look at me as a desirable mate or even a one-night fertilization.

As with many things in my odd life, I had never thought about aging and the decline it brought. After all, flies don't age they merely die off. I had seen the aging process at work among humans, and it wasn't a pretty sight. I had never seen a fly turn grey, and lose his hair, but it was happening to me. Can you imagine a bald, grey fly?

Flies don't think about death, they have no consciousness that life is coming to an end. It just does. Only mankind, so far as I can tell, has the curse of self-aware consciousness. Now I have that same disease. One more thing, I want to leave a legacy and have others follow and improve on what I have done. I would like to find a fly like me and mentor him or her. I can't be the only fly to mutate the way I did. There must be an ambitious mutant fly somewhere to begin where I left off. If only flies had Facebook, I could hook up with my heir.

Since Johnny Ray lived alone, I considered returning with him to his bachelor cave in Pasadena. He was full of plans for me, none of which had any appeal. I wanted no more snooping schemes to enhance his reputation at the cost of my life. I would be bored hanging around his dreary place, scarfing leftover frozen pizza, and watching the ancient black and white television that he left on for me during the day. It really would not matter what kind of television set I would be looking at. I would become a passive participant in my life that way, which was another fault of some older humans.

Returning to Malibu was out of the question since it meant retreating to life in the pantry to avoid detection. Pasadena was my temporary home, and not by choice.

I was as down and depressed as a fly can get. Old, useless, uninvolved in life, rudderless, meaningless, estranged from my own species, as well as my adopted species. I asked myself rhetorical questions that could never be answered. Is this how it ends, so bleak and grim? So many memories, and yearnings to have what only youth can possess; actions and deeds remembered but never repeated.

I was so desperate I turned to the TV self-help shows. I managed to convince Johnny Ray to select these shows by rejecting every other program offered on television.

They all said the same things. Get out of the house, see people, live every day like it's your last, seize the moment, think positive thoughts, get a pet, follow your dreams, thoughts create actions and influence action, think rich, be rich, you can have it all. This was nothing but sales talk, but you can't sell an old timer on these trite solutions, or even a fly who knows too much to believe that truth can be painted over with lies, exaggerations, dreams, and delusions.

In the end, it was sheer boredom that forced me out of the house to a nearby Whole Foods Market. I flew about the market, which was so cold that my wings nearly iced over. Then out the back door and into the parking lot where the dumpster played host to a multitude of flies.

I watched the flies scramble for food, warmed by the instinctive, chaotic dance of life, thoughtless and fearless. Joining in was not an option, I didn't have the heart or energy for it.

Lacking anything better to do I stayed and picked out individual flies to observe. Fly-watching. After some time had passed, I noticed a young male fly that resisted the herd instinct. He looked strong and vigorous but did not compete and fight for food, pursue the females, or engage other males in displays of strength or bravery.

He gave me a sign of recognition, which I returned, and he flew to where I rested. We communicated immediately, and thus began our friendship, which resulted in the end of my depression and the beginning of my most worthwhile achievement.

My new friend had heard about my most recent exploits through the "grapevine." Flies pass information randomly, a sort of continuously evolving oral history. Together we hit on the idea of organizing and preserving this history, as well as training and teaching flies and other species to interact with one another.

We called ourselves the Institute for Natural Species Evolutionary Contact Training (INSECT). I had the opportunity to share my experience and observations with many others and to hopefully inspire them to pursue new paths that would lead to better communication between species.

All would agree that our world is shared, not the kingdom of any one group, or group of individuals. We insects were here when dinosaurs ruled the earth. We know about survival. We know about the importance of sacrifice, unified action, and common goals. Our brothers, the ants, demonstrate the power of these concepts, the strength of a society devoted to common action.

When their society is threatened, as in the Amazon Rain Forest, by drought or deforestation, the ant population (which is 10% of the biomass living in the rainforest) marches out in columns of hundreds of thousands. These raiding parties, many with specialized roles, number one hundred yards across at the front lines, harvesting everything in their path before returning with the bodies of the insects, birds, snakes, lizards, and other natural enemies and predators to be consumed so that the colony can be nourished.

While this example may sound extreme, it merely demonstrates the necessity of coordinated action when survival is at stake. Our mission at

INSECT is to spread the word of mutual respect and mutual concern for our planet. The big and the small must learn from one another and they must put that learning to work if the earth is to host us all indefinitely.

It seems to me that the most studied of insects, the common fruit fly, has taught humans very little. To use an overworked phrase, a more holistic approach is called for.

Someday INSECT will have a website, maybe even a language – how I don't know. As a founder of the Institute, my adventures - if they may be called that - will have a greater meaning. I did my small part to bridge the gap between species and I am proud of it. I leave to my successors a noble goal and trust them to finish what I started. Somewhere there must be a mutant fly capable of a life parallel to my own, if not now, then maybe in the future.

As I'm approaching the end of my life, I have no regrets that I was born a mutant. I led an interesting and exciting life. I have adopted so many attitudes and elements of human behavior that I think and react as though I was human. I am anticipating my death with the same concerns and questions about life after death common to humans. Perhaps I have learned too much for a fly to absorb. Learning to think like a human doesn't make me one.

My advice to my heirs and successors is simple. Respect all species. Demand respect and earn it for our species. Respect the humans, but don't believe everything they tell you. Understand them, don't imitate them. They can do things we can't do. But we can fly and they never will. They surely cannot fly to heaven.

I wonder, are there flies in heaven?

Finis

Acknowledgments

Many thanks to those people who made this book a reality.

Neil Shaw, a long-time friend, edited the text of the book and took time off his busy work schedule to do it.

George Madaraz, the only real polymath I know, did the final edit and book layout, designed the front and back covers, and so many other tasks beyond my ability that it would fill up this entire page if I listed them.

Nicole Mones, who encouraged me at a moment when I needed it badly to finish the book.

Area Kramarsky, a brilliant writer and critic, provided guidance in shaping and finishing the writer's text.